A Tiger
in Red Weather

By John Wyllie

A TIGER IN RED WEATHER
THE KILLER BREATH
A POCKET FULL OF DEAD
DEATH IS A DRUM . . . BEATING FOREVER
TO CATCH A VIPER
THE BUTTERFLY FLOOD
SKULL STILL BONE
THE GOODLY SEED
DOWN WILL COME THE SKY
RIOT
JOHNNY PURPLE

A Tiger
in Red Weather

JOHN WYLLIE

PUBLISHED FOR THE CRIME CLUB BY

DOUBLEDAY & COMPANY, INC.

GARDEN CITY, NEW YORK

1980

ISBN: 0-385-15954-4
Library of Congress Catalog Card Number 79-6285
Copyright © 1980 by John Wyllie

For Malcolm

The parts of this story which deal with the history of the Ancient Empire of Mali and its great wealth are authenticated by a variety of history books and the writings of Arab historians who lived in the thirteenth century. Otherwise it is a work of fiction and any resemblance between the characters and any persons living or dead can only be a coincidence.

A Tiger
in Red Weather

The man, wearing a genet-skin apron and carrying a dane gun, was a hunter so the sight of blood stimulated his interest as its smell stimulates the interest of other predators. The way the blood was smeared on the rocks indicated that, whatever the creature was, it was dragging itself along the ground. Or, perhaps, it was being dragged because, in one or two shallow pools of dust, there were traces of what might have been identifiable as paw marks had the outlines not been smudged by wind-blown sand. The shallow indentations had also been partly obliterated by deep furrows which suggested that whatever it was that was being dragged was heavy; heavier than even the largest gazelle, which the hunter could still find in the Sahelian scrub desert surrounding the rocky outcrop where the trail began. This puzzled the man because there was no game that heavy in this territory.

The landscape looked like a backdrop for some bizarre play in which all life was wiped out because it needed water to survive and there was none. It also grew more sinister as the sun moved towards the western horizon lengthening the shadows on the slabs of rock and patches of sand by jagged piles of boulders and abrupt, butte-like insulbergs.

It was land which had once supported a human community until herds of goats, camels and cattle had grazed it bare right down to a rocky skeleton that was thinly and sporadically fleshed with dust in which there grew a few spiky acacia bushes.

Then the hunter found the mangled body of a white woman with black hair buried beneath a small cairn of stones in a shallow pit of sand about a mile from the point where the trail of blood had started.

The only white woman the hunter knew of for hundreds of miles in any direction was in the small town of Norenga. However, she had long red hair. He knew that because, having refused to believe that such a phenomenon could exist, he had been taken to see her.

That woman was no bigger than a mouse, he remembered. This one was large, fat and now as shapeless as if a giant had pounded her to death with the side of his fist or, perhaps, as if she had fallen onto the slab of rock from a great height.

The hunter was loath to touch the body but moved downwind of it. There he sniffed the air and decided that the kill was fresh. It probably had lain in its shallow grave only overnight.

He covered the body again with rocks and turned and ran towards a road which lay a couple of miles to the east. He then ran on down the road until a truck, coming from the frontier with Transniger, overtook him and gave him a lift into Norenga.

He decided not to tell anyone of his discovery until he could speak with the small white doctor who was married to the mouse-like woman with red hair.

The doctor was a good man. Everybody said so but the hunter knew how good he was from his own experience. For he had been attacked, once, by a lion and had been given up for dead before the doctor had started to work on him. Indeed, even today, when he showed people the scars, they all said that the doctor's "medicine" had clearly been more potent than any which might have been used by the hunter's enemies to cause the lion to attack him. It was, therefore, everyone said, most important that he preserve his relationship with such a clever man.

So, the doctor was a good man and would know, better than any other, what he should do about his discovery of the body of the fat white woman, who looked as if she might have fallen from the sky to split open on the rocks.

CHAPTER ONE

*"You cannot say he is an animal because no animal is so
bad as he."*

Dr. Quarshie took a long pull at his glass of beer without removing his eyes from the American ambassador, who was saying, "I'm afraid we don't know very much, Doctor. A man of your experience, however, must be accustomed to having people tell him that at the outset of an investigation into a mysterious death."

The ambassador was referring to the half-dozen murder cases which Quarshie had investigated in the past three or four years.

"The first time we met, you remember, you were trying to discover the identity of a white man who had, all too literally, lost his head. He turned out to be a U.S. national. This time there is no problem of identification. Miss Martha Solveig was not only an American but really quite well known in certain circles in our society."

Quarshie had learned of Miss Solveig's death only a couple of hours earlier when he answered the telephone in his surgery and had found Colonel Jedawi, Akhana's President, on the other end of the line.

As usual the colonel had not wasted any words. "I've got a nice job for you, Doctor," he said as if he were doing Quarshie a favour. "The American ambassador has just phoned to say that an American citizen has been found dead, in peculiar circumstances, on our border with Transniger. I spoke with Ephraim Osomany, the D.O. up there, on our short-wave link and he told me that he doesn't have any doubt that she came to . . . ah . . . a sticky end. Of course, we have to do something about it."

A royal command. Nor had the ambassador bothered to enquire whether Quarshie had consented to undertake the investigation. He had apparently assumed that the doctor's presence at the embassy indicated that he had.

Since it was four o'clock in the afternoon the ambassador only toyed with his beer while he "filled Quarshie in" on the little he knew about the dead woman.

"She wrote books, Doctor," he explained, "romantic ones about young people who live in out-of-the-way places. Though, in my opinion and the opinion of quite a number of other people, her stories were excessively melodramatic, she was scrupulous about background detail. Currently she was working on a story about two young people who are supposed to be employed in Africa in the Peace Corps. So she came out here and went up north to get local colour for the book. She was also a journalist and she made her fact-finding trips pay a bonus by writing features for syndication in various women's magazines in our country."

The ambassador paused and sipped his beer before adding, "But don't let that thumbnail sketch lead you to think of her just as some sort of empty-headed, female gossip writer. I do not like her work but after she came through here and I met her a couple of times I decided that her seeming concern with trivialities and platitudes was a façade designed to conceal a different woman with sharp wits and determination. That is about all I can tell you. However, you will, no doubt, find that the people in Norenga had learned a lot more about her because she had been living up there for almost two months—as you know, I'm sure, it's a very small community. I shall, of course, get a more complete report on her from the people at home as soon as I can and I will let you see it when it arrives. Do you have any questions?"

Quarshie thought of another order he had received from Jedawi: it was that he treat his investigations as being of great importance from the diplomatic point of view. He had been told to step very carefully. So, after weighing his words, he asked casually, "Can you say, sir, whether or not she might have been employed in clandestine activities?"

The ambassador smiled. "You mean might her writing be some sort of cover for work done for the CIA? I am afraid the old saw about people looking for a red under every bed has been replaced by the idea that there is a CIA man under every divan."

Quarshie wanted to say that he didn't mean that she might have been a CIA operative but exactly what he had said: had she been employed in clandestine activities. He had learned, however, that in diplomacy one behaves as dogs do in a dog fight. When one dog goes belly-up the other waits for it to make another move before attacking again, so he let the ambassador get away with his evasion and nodded gravely.

The ambassador said, "I have not been presented with any evidence to that effect. But before giving you a categorical answer perhaps I had better wait for the dossier from Washington. However, if during your investigation you turn up anything which makes you suspicious I would be grateful if you would check with me immediately. Right?"

In other words, Quarshie thought, either the ambassador knew more than he was saying, or he suspected something. Most diplomats, he supposed, learned young that the less you committed yourself, the less you could be held accountable for.

So Quarshie let that answer rest, requested Miss Solveig's passport number, found a picture of her on the dust wrapper on one of her books, which was in the U. S. Information Service's library, and was given copies of a couple of the magazine articles she had written.

Then, as he was taking his leave of him, the ambassador said, "I nearly forgot to give you a message, Doctor. Your friend, the French ambassador, asked that you drop in and see him before you go north. I was talking to the old man earlier. You know, he has a very high opinion of you and that is an accolade few men ever win because he is quite ruthlessly critical of most people." There was a not very well concealed element of personal feeling in the ambassador's words and Quarshie wondered what the old Frenchman had been up to to cause his fellow diplomat to make a statement like that. "*Je suis un taquin, tu sais, mon ami,*" the old man had once told him. "Jus' I tease a ver' little, you understand? It is for fun."

Obviously the "fun" could hurt but the foreign ambassadors

in Akhana had to put up with it because the old Frenchman knew more about West Africa than all the rest of them put together and gave them very wise guidance.

"Coincidence, Quarshie, have a false reputation, *tu sais?* It is talk about by everybody like it is a miracle every time it 'appen." The French ambassador put his head on one side and his white hair, lit by a lamp behind him, made a shining aureole around his skull. "But it is something which come along every day. For instance, the job you will do for McKechney," he was speaking of the American ambassador, "is fitting ver' nicely with a little job I would like you to do for me."

Quarshie smiled and said, "You don't fool me for one minute, Jules. You make things happen to suit your needs and then you call it coincidence. Just who was it who put the idea in McKechney's mind that I would be the right man for this job?"

With Mrs. Quarshie, the two men were sitting in the library of the ambassador's residence in Port St. Mary, the capital of Akhana. It was the room in which the old Frenchman spent most of his time when he was not engaged in his official duties and it contained one of the most complete collections of books to be found anywhere in the world on the history, anthropology, ethnology, flora and fauna of West Africa.

The room was lit by only one small standard lamp with a red silk shade. It stood near the ambassador's left shoulder and its light threw his head and shoulders into silhouette each time he leaned forward, as he did now.

"*Bon.* So I play a little bit the *deus ex machina,* my friend," he said with a shrug, "but it is a fact, you know, that I receive this letter, in the diplomatic bag, from the Quay D'Orsay jus' this morning before I get the alarm call from McKechney. And that is really a coincidence. It is telling me that the Quai, or rather the Sûreté, is worry about a certain Monsieur André Grevier. He is a man who have many *nom d'emprunt* . . . how you say it in English, Quarshie?"

"Alias, I guess." Quarshie had acquired his fluency in French and English in Canada, where he had studied medicine.

"Ah, in French we can say the same. So, I suppose somebody in the Sûreté is finding that he have a dossier on this man which is still open and he wish to close it. The last time anyone hear of this Grevier he has been see by someone who recognise him at the *frontière* up north between Akhana and Transniger, near Norenga." He turned a page or two of the document on his desk and then, speaking to Mrs. Quarshie, he told her, "He is not a nice man, this Grevier, Prudence. That is from his record. Though this document also say that he can be ver' charming, quite the, how you call it, con man, no? Now I want to . . ."

A roll of thunder in hot and humid pursuit of others, which had been shaking the air all evening in a most unseasonal storm, obliterated the ambassador's next words as well as all the other sounds of the tropical night. After it had passed away northwards and while the ambassador sent his steward, Alphonse, for more beer for Quarshie, there followed a few moments, outside, of brooding silence that was soon shattered by a blast of wind that slammed jalousie shutters all over the building and drove big heavy leaves, twigs, dust and insects against the screen netting outside the windows.

In the immediate wake of the storm came a delightful coolness and the patter of a sprinkling of rain on the corrugated iron roof over the library. There was also an exciting smell of damp soil which seemed to act on the heavens like the scent of a bitch in heat acts on a pack of dogs and led to the arrival of a rampaging line squall. It swept in, furiously, off the ocean and the rain hammered Port St. Mary's buildings and roadways. The deluge, driven by the frantic impulse of the wind, scourged the windows and made a noise on the roof like the wild applause of a vast, hysterical crowd. It also made conversation impossible and Mrs. Quarshie sat back in her chair and looked at her husband and the ambassador through half-closed eyes.

They were, she decided, the two men who, in recent years, had had the greatest effect on her life. They were also the two with whom she felt the safest and the most comfortable.

The contrast between them, at the physical and emotional level, was, however, about as great as it could be.

Quarshie was huge and black; the ambassador was small, as lean as a whippet and the fairness of his skin was emphasised by the whiteness of his hair.

Quarshie's movements were measured and deliberate. The ambassador, by contrast, was constantly in motion. Everything he said was given added value by the gestures he made. It was as if his words were different instruments in an orchestra and he conducted them to increase or diminish their emphasis.

Of course the two men had similarities, as well. Though one was a doctor and the other a diplomat they both made study of their fellow men their greatest concern because it was an integral part of their professions. There was, however, Mrs. Quarshie thought, a little more acid in the ambassador's view of humanity than there was in Quarshie's, so that the Frenchman's judgements were etched more sharply than her husband's. The old man had a mordant sense of humour and used it quite often as a weapon with which he drew blood.

Quarshie, for all his size and muscle, or perhaps because of it, knowing that he had the strength to kill with his bare hands . . . he had done so, once . . . was a very gentle man. He was not, however, humourless; he could and did laugh as often as the next man. He believed that murder was something which should earn its perpetrator a swift reprisal as it had before the arrival of white men in Africa. To most Africans life was sacred and it could be taken only in battle for a just cause or as an offering to the gods, or the ancestors. Murder, for any kind of material gain, was the most heinous offense of all.

As the force of the squall abated Mrs. Quarshie came to the conclusion that her man was easier to love than the ambassador though her affection for the older man was still very strong.

"So, I am saying, when this *tempête* is breaking, André Grevier is a *pied noire,* a white man born and bring up in North Africa and he is an officer in the army until he is kick out. He is, it say here, very bad news to black man and even more bad news to black women. He is"—the ambassador looked for a word, found it and used it—"*bestial*. But he is also a ver' good *chasseur* and a champion with a *carabine,* a gun. When he shoot, he shoot ver' straight and any time *il tire*"—the ambassador aimed and fired an imaginary gun—"pouf . . . his *objectif* fall down dead. Also he is a ver' good man to be in charge of a job because every man who is work for him is fear him too much and work like the devil. The man from the Quay send me a copy of this monsieur's confidential file. He is, it say in the file"—and the ambassador numbered the points on his fingers— "*contrabandier,* you call it smuggler, no? *Escroc,* that is swindler, thief and he is maybe *assassin,* but this is not prove. Also, with a gang, who is all coming from the back streets of Oran, Algier, Casablanca and Bizerte, he is specialist, we think, for catching little black and Arab girls and selling them to people who buy this kind of *merchandise.* Is it enough? Do you know now why, maybe, it is time the dossier is close on the man? You cannot say he is an animal because no animal is so bad as he. You must get him, Quarshie."

CHAPTER TWO

". . . he believes she was 'stoned to death.'"

From the typically African township that Quarshie had known twenty years earlier when, as a newly qualified doctor, he had been posted to the neighbouring town of Bonga, he found that Norenga had become something approaching a twentieth-century city.

There were buildings, now, which stood three or four stories high, and though the central market, which had originally given the town its importance, was still there, it had new competition in the form of two air-conditioned supermarkets. When Quarshie had been the medical officer in the district and had wanted to fill the gas tank of his car the fuel had been pumped into it by hand from a transparent cylinder balanced on the top of a sixty-gallon drum. Now, Esso, Caltex, Agip, BP and Shell filling stations displayed signs proclaiming their proprietary interests.

Looking at this noisy and blatantly commercial "progress" as they drove down the main street, Quarshie remembered a statement that had been made by one of the world's wisest men, who has a gift for succinct summarisation. The man had said, "In dealing with underdeveloped countries the main objective of the technologically proficient West has been to change a taste for good, clean water into a taste for Coca-Cola."

Quarshie repeated the phrase for Mrs. Quarshie, who sat beside him in the car as they headed towards the Government Rest House to drop off their bags and wash some of the red dust off their skins.

She nodded, reflected and then asked, "How long did it take us to drive up here from the coast?"

"About twelve hours."

"And how long would it have taken us to do the journey on foot before the Coca-Cola salesmen and their friends visited Akhana?"

"Twenty to twenty-five days."

"So, without help, we now take a twentieth of the time to travel the same distance that they did on foot with several other men to carry their baggage for them."

"Yes, but to what purpose?"

"Life is short, we need to make the most of our time."

"But don't we waste most of it, anyway?"

"Ah, that's not the fault of the people who invent machines but because people have not been taught to use them properly. All these things have come too quickly and too suddenly."

The district officer, Ephraim Osomany, when they eventually got to see him, was also feeling that things were coming too quickly and suddenly.

Quarshie was as surprised by the changes that had come over Osomany as he had been about the changes that had taken place in the town. He and the district officer had been at the University College together in the days before Akhana had become independent. They had both been on the college boxing team, Quarshie as a heavyweight, Ephraim as a middleweight. Both had also made a habit of winning, Quarshie by playing a waiting game, maintaining an almost impenetrable defence and hitting hard and fast when his opponent dropped his guard. Ephraim had always been the aggressor, going energetically on the offensive from the first bell.

Now, the frustrations involved in "development" had gotten to Ephraim and had worn him down, taking the edge off his natural enthusiasms and sapping his energy. At root the difference between the two men was that Quarshie husbanded his vitality so he always had something in reserve. Ephraim spent his furiously until he ran out of it.

His problems in Norenga had increased the load on his time without giving him any extra equipment, either physical or mental, to cope with it.

In short, he was a harassed man.

For, as he explained, besides having to deal with the administrative problems of Norenga there had been a major upheaval in the wider district that was under his control, caused by the

construction of a dam almost a hundred miles south. It had ne-
cessitated the relocation of several villages because their sites
were going to be converted into a lake.

The villagers had not only resented being made to move, he
told the Quarshies, but had taken to dying to register their dis-
pleasure. It was a form of protest which mostly involved the
old people who were totally unable to adapt to being wrenched
from places which contained the bones and therefore the spirits
of their ancestors. To them it was a matter of the desecration of
sanctified land, as the conversion of St. Patrick's Cathedral or
of Westminster Abbey into a power station would be to those
people who felt that each place had been made sacred by all
those who had worshipped there.

"Some people," Ephraim said, "have even been calling me a
murderer."

He threw up his hands in despair and said, "And the people
I have to deal with in the expat community! They are all crazy,
or crooks, or both. But you will see that tomorrow. It's Christmas Day and you will be invited. You know what it is supposed
to mean, don't you? Peace, good will on earth, all that. Every
year they have a party and a Christmas tree, specially flown out
from Germany, at Dr. Levitsky's expense. Why the doctor isn't
even a Christian . . . but he goes through it all for his wife's
sake.

"They all are peculiar, except the doctor—and even he has to
be a bit unbalanced to treat his wife the way he does. You'll
see. With you two, there will be ten of us there. The doctor will
insist you come and since you and he are going to have to work
together, Sam, you had better get off on a good footing with
him."

"Ten," Quarshie was surprised. "Who all are going to be
there?"

"Well"—Ephraim wrote the names down on a pad as he
spoke them—"there is Dr. Levitsky and his wife, Hanna."

"But, he's not one of the really crazy ones, you say?"

"Well, not really. Of course, you could say he works like a
lunatic but I don't suppose that makes him one. One thing

about him is clear—the people here love him and take their problems to him rather than me. The wife? You would not believe me if I told you about her so I will wait until you meet her."

The pen Ephraim was using ran out of ink and he threw it away irritably. "Then there is Percy Courtney-Beauchamp, pronounced Beecham. He does not make life any easier for me because he used to be the chief commissioner for the whole Northern Territories. It must have been about a thousand years ago because he is over eighty. He retired here and is a world authority on the history and artifacts of the reign of the Malian Emperor, Mansa Musah, who died, Percy has told me a dozen times, around 1385. That was a little before the English murdered one of their kings—was it Richard the Second? They taught us about him at school but not about Mansa Musah."

"I wonder Jules did not tell us about Mr. Courtney-Beauchamp," Mrs. Quarshie said.

"Jealousy . . . experts are often jealous of each other. Man was born to compete whether it is in academic pursuits or in the boxing ring. Right, Ephraim?"

"Or in how you administer a piece of territory. I would like to get him off my back for just a few days. He is always dropping in and to listen to him you'd think he was still the chief commissioner." Ephraim shook his head, sighed and allowed a depressed silence to settle over the room.

"So that's three out of ten." Quarshie prodded him.

"Then there is a fairly normal young black couple from the U.S. They don't much like what they see here of educated black people—it confirms, I suspect, their worst fears. With you and Levitsky it will mean that there will be four doctors in the neighbourhood. They are here on some kind of foundation grant studying nutrition, although his real specialisation is pediatrics. She is the nutritionist.

"Then there is a character called Temple. He's from London, East Ham. Another 'old coaster' like Percy but from the other end of the social scale. He tells everyone to call him 'Shirley' because that was the nickname they gave him in the army. He was, I think, a sergeant in the West African Frontier Force. He married one of our people, took his discharge in Akhana and settled. He runs a branch of a big British contracting outfit up here building roads and bridges. And I can tell you he is one I wouldn't let slip around behind my back any time I was in trouble. Finally, there is a Monsieur René Dupré in town. He comes and goes. He claims to be a geologist working up on the other side of the frontier in Transniger. He is supposed to be looking for uranium. I don't know why, but I don't buy that story. He and Shirley make a bright pair. So, that's seven. With us three it makes ten."

"And what about Miss Solveig?"

"She won't be at the party. Sorry, that was in bad taste."

"But she would have been if she had been alive?"

"Most certainly. She would have been one of the leading lights of our happy little band. She had already started spending money on the celebrations."

"Did you know her well?"

Ephraim looked at the ends of his fingers and then out of the window. After a long time and in a subdued voice he replied, "I did. Very well. You will find out about it soon enough so I can only make things look bad for myself by sitting on the information. My wife and I separated two years ago and took a tribal custom divorce. So there was nothing to stop my friendship with Martha from developing and coming to . . . to full bloom."

"She told me she had always wanted to find out what it was like to 'get laid,' I think she said, by a black. For my part I have always wondered what it would be like to share my mattress with a white woman."

"And how was it?" The question came from Mrs. Quarshie and she surprised herself as much as she surprised the two men by asking it.

"Good. But different." Mrs. Quarshie wanted to ask in what way but found the words would not come. Ephraim wanted to add to his statement, too, and did so after a moment. "She had some funny ideas about the sort of things . . ." he paused, then said carefully, "men and women can do together."

Mrs. Quarshie still wanted to go further but after she had remained silent for quite a while looking for the words she needed Quarshie took the initiative away from her.

"Aside from her bedtime behaviour," he asked, "what kind of woman was she? And how was she killed?"

"Dr. Levitsky did the P.M. He will tell you in detail what he found. But in three words he believes she was 'stoned to death.'" Mrs. Quarshie let out a little gasp. "What kind of woman? Pretty unusual. She liked to be independent. She liked to have lots of money and lots of things she could buy with it."

"Did she buy you?"

They looked like boxers now, Mrs. Quarshie thought, with her husband on the offensive and Ephraim in a corner.

"She gave me some presents." Quarshie backed off after that admission and waited. It was a sparring match more than a fight. "Also I helped her to find other things that she wanted. She was always looking for bargains, African sculpture, Ashanti gold weights—antiquities, she called them—Marie Louise silver coins, wood carvings, bronze castings, the lot. Gold ornaments, too. And provided she thought she was onto 'a good deal' she would go after it whatever it cost. The Hausa traders really respected her. She drove a hard bargain, not like most expats and tourists."

"And Dr. Levitsky, let's go back to him. I intend to go and see him when we leave here. Is there anything about him that I should know?"

"I don't know what his original nationality was but now he has British papers. He calls himself and his wife lapsed Jews. He was in the British Army Medical Corps during the war and picked his wife up right out of a concentration camp. That's all I know. He never talks about himself. He just works like mad, plays a guitar and sings sad songs under the moon."

"And Miss Solveig, has anyone started to make any investigations? Who reported finding her body and would he be available to take me to the place?"

"Yes, to your last question. He is an old hunter and I told him to stay around. He came in in a hurry after making the discovery and reported it to Dr. Levitsky, who told me and we went out, with the hunter and a couple of policemen, to bring her in. She was a . . . she was a mess. The man who killed her must have been a maniac."

"How far out of Norenga was the body found?"

"In scrub desert west of mile forty-two."

"Any idea why she was there?"

"None at all. We had to walk almost two miles from the road to reach the place."

"No tyre tracks?"

"The ground is mostly slabs of rock and shale. And where there is sand it is pretty fine so it blows about a lot. Not ideal tracking country."

"So there were no marks of any kind that might suggest what happened?"

"The hunter said that she had been dragged quite a long way by something which could have had four or more legs. She had left a trail of blood. It was all very nasty. The hunter has the opinion now that the supernatural had a hand in it. She had had some kind of row with a fetisher. She told me a little about it. He had a couple of little wooden fertility dolls that were the real thing, but he wouldn't part with them. She bargained with him for a long time. Finally, she put down what, by local standards, was an astronomical sum of money and simply snatched the little figures and walked off with them. There was talk in the market that the fetisher had put a curse on her.

"I haven't had time to do any real investigation myself and something like this is away beyond the capabilities of the local police. When the President said you would be coming on the day we brought in the body I told the police to lock up the bungalow she had been living in, which belongs to my assistant, who is away on leave, and to put a guard on it, night and day, because I thought you would want to look it over."

"Yes, fine. Get someone to take a message over to tell them

we are coming right away. After that we will go to the hospital and contact Levitsky."

"And you'll be at the Christmas party, tomorrow, eh? It's quite a . . . a dramatic spectacle. And it will help to cement your relationship with Dr. Levitsky and give you an understanding of the kind of problems he has to face."

Outside in the sun Mrs. Quarshie looked around at the blue sky and a jacaranda tree which was competing by flaunting its amethyst-coloured blooms against it. There was also a white cow with long horns lazily stretching its neck to pull straw out of a thatched roof and a very small boy who came running to beat it with a stick. Everything was dry and dusty and brown . . . and quite normal. She felt reassured because listening to Ephraim she had begun to feel that she was losing contact with reality.

CHAPTER THREE

". . . she was a grade-A bitch . . ."

The police corporal saluted Quarshie as if the doctor were carrying out a parade-ground inspection.

Quarshie said, "Good afternoon, Corporal. Is the inspector here?"

"He no fit come, sah. Send say you gettum key, sah, make you go for inside."

As they followed the man to the door of the small bungalow Quarshie told his wife softly, "That probably means the inspector is antagonistic. Another case of the competitive instinct I was talking about. I will have to go and see him . . . I don't want any ruffled feathers around here. We are going to need everyone's co-operation. On second thought, we'll go and see him together. Your winning ways will probably work better with him than any charm I can turn on. If you go alone, however, he may feel slighted."

The house which Martha Solveig had occupied had a living room, a bedroom, a toilet and shower and a wide verandah which reached around it on three sides. There was an outside kitchen built separately from the main structure but joined to it by a mosquito-netted passageway, and, a hundred feet farther away, there was very simple accommodation for a cook-houseboy and a gardener-handy man.

"Catch man for dat place, dere?" Quarshie asked the corporal and pointed towards the servants' quarters.

"Yessah, catch."

"Make you go axum come here, one time."

The corporal unlocked the back door and went to do Quarshie's bidding.

After glancing around Quarshie told his wife, "You take the bedroom and bathroom, Prudence. I'll take this room. O.K.?"

Mrs. Quarshie shook her head in housewifely despair and said, "The dust. Look at it, in just four days."

Quarshie, who was gazing at the desk that stood in front of a window, did not respond immediately. Then he said, "But in some places it hasn't lain undisturbed all that time. Here"—and he pointed. Beside a portable typewriter there was a clear rectangle in the dust. He traced it with his finger. "See? Something was lying here until quite recently. Ephraim said they left to examine the body the morning after the old hunter came in and reported finding it. Suppose they got back here at noon and then he contacted Jedawi and, I suppose, the American ambassador. That would have taken him, given the condition of the telephone services, until late in the afternoon. So this place could have been without a guard from the time Martha left until the following evening." He took the key out of the lock in the front door and examined it. "This is the simplest kind of thing you can imagine." He waved it at Mrs. Quarshie before slipping it into the lock again. "I would bet that there are hundreds like it in Norenga." He went back and stared at the table with the telltale mark on it. "Of course what sat there could have been there a long time. I mean, it wasn't something she put there just before she left."

"A book?" Mrs. Quarshie hazarded.

"Beside the typewriter more likely something which held her papers, a big envelope or file."

The corporal came back with a youngish man dressed in a starched white jacket and khaki shorts and a much older man whose khaki shirt and pants were covered with patches and mends but were neat and clean.

"This he be cook-houseboy, sah. The old man he garden boy."

"Catch pidgin?"

The corporal addressed the two men in the local language and they both shook their heads, though the cook-houseboy made some response.

"Cook-houseboy, he name Naga, sah, say he catch pidgin, small, small."

"Is there one amongst you who hears Hausa?" Quarshie asked in that language.

The corporal and the cook-houseboy both answered together, "Peace be on you sir, I do."

Quarshie continued in that language:

"When did the white woman leave the house? Was it on the
same day that they brought her back? Early in the morning,
perhaps?"

"No, sir," the cook-houseboy replied, "nor the day before,
but the day before that, Kissim day." The days of the week
were named for the place where the principal market for that
day took place. There were five small market towns in the cir-
cuit so the local week was measured in segments of five days.

"Do you know where she went?"

"No, sir."

"Did she have a car?"

"No, sir. She had one man who drives a taxi. She always
made arrangements with him, or she sent me to fetch him. I
have a bicycle."

Quarshie gave Mrs. Quarshie the gist of the conversation.

"You could fetch the taxi man?" Quarshie asked the "boy."

"Yes, sir. Now?"

"Soon. First, did the lady usually keep anything on this table
beside the writing machine?"

"Always, sir. A thing with much paper in it. Thick like this."
The young man demonstrated with the forefinger and thumb on
his right hand.

"Used paper, or clean paper?"

"Used paper. The clean paper is there beside the books."

"Was the used paper there when the lady went away?"

"It was not."

"When did you last dust in here?"

"I never dust. The lady said I did not do it properly. She did
it, herself."

"Did she give you much trouble?"

The "boy" wriggled his toes and, after a slight pause, said,
"She was a woman in whom there lived a great impatience."

"Did the lady have many visitors?"

"Yes, sir."

"Do you know any of them?"

"I would know them again if I saw them, but not who they are."

"White men and black men?"

"As you say, sir, both."

"Did any of them stay with the lady? I mean lie with her."

"Yes, sir. One who was white and one who was black."

"Did you see anyone come to this house after the lady went away?"

"The second night when the lady did not come back I travelled to my village to see my mother. When I was here I did not see anyone. Should I ask the old one, sir, whether he saw anybody?"

"He was here when you travelled?"

"He was, sir."

"Then do you speak with him and ask him that question." The "boy" spoke with the gardener in their own language. Then he turned back to Quarshie and said, "He did not see anyone, sir. But he woke in the night and heard a car driving away, though he did not hear it arrive."

"Corporal, has anyone come to visit this house while you have been guarding it?"

"Yes, sir, the old one who was the chief commissioner came. When he saw me on guard he said it was good, that everything would be safe. Also the white doctor came. He said he needed the lady's passport. I was with him all the time. He looked everywhere but he could not find it."

"Thank you." To the "boy" he repeated the same words and 'added, "Now fetch the taxi man, please." To the corporal he said, "Tell the old one he can go and you wait outside."

Alone with his wife Quarshie said, "Well . . . we have already opened up doors to all kinds of possibilities. The taxi man should have some useful information, too. While we wait for him we'll look around and see what else there is which might be interesting."

At the end of about an hour the most obvious discrepancy in the tally of what they might have expected to find was the kind of data a writer might keep when she was out gathering material for a book, or for newspaper articles. There was not a scrap of paper, anywhere, with notes on it.

Each of them, however, found items of interest.

The material which Quarshie found was in the dozen or so paperbacks which stood on the shelf beside the unused paper. Both the books' titles and the notes scribbled in their margins suggested that Martha was seriously interested in a certain phase of early West African history and, surprisingly for a woman who had travelled all over the world alone, she was interested in herself and her reasons for being a solitary.

As he read her comments and the marked passages in the books, Quarshie saw her as, perhaps, she saw herself. She was a woman on the run. But she was not, it seemed, running blindly and she evidently hoped that she was not running away from something but towards a goal of some sort.

The notes in the margins made the contents of the books a sort of dialogue between Martha Solveig and the books' authors. Sometimes she agreed with them quite emphatically, then she underlined statements and wrote "Oh yes" beside them. On other occasions she argued quite hotly. For example, when a writer said, "The alienated person must be as out of touch with himself as he is with the people around him," she had written, "Why? Why, though I am out of touch with myself, should I be out of touch with other people? That's like saying that because I cannot play a piano I cannot appreciate the work of people who can." And when another writer whose book was anonymous wrote, "And perhaps it is because of the contempt we feel for the pasty white bodies and their owners who pass, like milk bottles on a conveyor belt, through our hands, that there are so many coloured ponces, for after the curds and whey of European flesh, warm sepias and ebonies must inevitably tickle our palates." She had written in the margin, "That's the truth, sister, that's the truth."

Then there were books with such titles as *Ancient Ghana and Mali, Old Africa Rediscovered* and *The Gold Trade of the Moors*. It was, in fact, the last book which spoke most truly for

Martha's greatest interest. One sentence she had underlined read, "The rulers of ancient Ghana and Mali derived their income from controlling the routes to the sources of gold." Another read, "Around 1320 A.D. in the treasures of Mali there was a single bar of gold weighing three hundred and eighty pounds." And she had also found the following statement interesting: "The gold of Mali reached Egypt, the Mahgrib and even Europe by being transported across the desert in heavily guarded caravans."

However, it was Mrs. Quarshie's find which really caused the greatest sensation.

She had hunted slowly and methodically through Martha's not very extensive wardrobe and the two drawers in a chest, in which all the others were empty, and had turned to another chest with a mirror on it which Martha had evidently used as a dressing table. She had wrinkled her nose at all the cosmetics which lay around on the top of it but she had painstakingly examined each jar of cream, pushing her finger down into it to see if it contained anything other than it should. Having drawn a blank in all of them, she had casually picked up the hairbrush which was faced with a rubber pad containing very hard bristles and was surprised to find how heavy it was, though probably only a woman would have noticed the fact.

With an anticipatory sense of excitement she had used a long steel nail file to prise the rubber out of its seating. Then she had called softly to Quarshie.

Though she had not raised her voice Quarshie caught the urgency in her tone and joined her at once.

On the top of the chest of drawers in front of her she had spilled from the head of the brush three heavy gold medallions with curious designs in relief on one side of them.

When he stood beside her she looked up at him with her eyes very wide and in a slightly shaky tone of voice she said, "They were hidden in the hairbrush."

Quarshie picked them up, in turn, weighing them in the palm of his hand. Together they would have turned the scales at five or six ounces and they were evidently very old.

Quarshie said, "How clever of you to think of looking there. I wonder where she got them. We had better give them to Ephraim to put in a safe. No"—he frowned—"no." Turning the medallions over in his hand, he concluded, slowly, "How do we know Ephraim was telling the truth, or even part of it, about his relationship with Martha?"

A car drove up and Quarshie slipped the medallions into his pocket, saying, "What we do with them is going to need more thought. That will be the taxi driver. We must go and talk to him."

The man who met them on the verandah was much younger than Quarshie had expected and he spoke fluent English.

Before Quarshie could utter a word the young man said, "Are you the real Dr. Quarshie, sir? I can see you are. You are welcome, sir. Will you use my taxi, sir?"

"How do you know who I am?"

"I read a lot, sir. I wanted to go to university but there is no work for men with a university education so it is a waste of time. I told my father to buy me a taxi instead of sending me for more schooling. In a year I shall be able to buy another taxi. Then I will buy a lorry. Transport is good business, sir. Before long I shall be rich, then I shall be able to study because I like to study. Already the one who was chief commissioner lends me books."

"Then you know him?"

"When he wants a taxi he calls for me, sir." It was a simple statement, but it was loaded with pride. "Like you will, sir."

Quarshie smiled. "Sometimes, perhaps. I have my own car, but perhaps you will be able to drive my wife when I have something else to do."

"That will be a great pleasure, madam. I know every house in the town and everybody who lives there."

"Good," Quarshie told him. "Now, I believe you drove for the lady who was living here?"

"Yes, sir. Everywhere. All the time."

"Was she a good person to drive for?"

The young man hesitated, not sure what kind of response

was expected of him and afraid he might lose custom by saying the wrong thing.

"For instance, did she pay you well?"

"Not like white strangers usually do, sir. No more than I get from the people who live here. But she was a very clever lady and she knew many things."

"Where did you take her? I mean who did she go to see?"

"To many people, sir. Some who were my brothers and sisters"—he was speaking of the people who belonged to his tribe—"and some who were not. She also went to see other whites."

"To the doctor?"

"Often, sir. The doctor's lady liked to see her very much."

"How do you know that?"

"By the greeting she always gave her. It was the kind of greeting a woman gives a man. The lady who lived here was like a man in much that she did."

"Who else did she see?"

"The big man who lends me books, the white. He lives outside the town and has a big music machine in his garden. She went often to listen to music with him. Always at night. When she went out it was usually at night."

"And you had to wait for her?"

"Mostly, but not always."

"So, sometimes she stayed the whole night."

"Or the man she was visiting brought her home afterwards."

"But sometimes she did stay?"

Again there was a slight hesitation before the young man answered, "Yes, sir. Sometimes."

"With whom did she spend the whole night? And I wish you to answer truthfully. I shall only be angry if what you tell me is untrue, understand?"

"Yes, sir. Sometimes I would leave her at the house of the one who comes from the other side of the frontier. They say he is French. Then I would go back in the morning very early to fetch her."

"Did you do the same thing when you went to the house of the district officer?"

"You have been here only three hours, I saw you come, and you know that already? Indeed you are *the* Dr. Quarshie, who they sing about and from whom nothing is hidden."

"Was there anyone else she stayed with?"

"No, sir, not that I know about."

"Did she ever take a different taxi driver?"

"If she had she would have been cheating me. She made me give her a special price because she made me a promise that she will never use another driver."

"How did other people like her, do you know?"

"I think some were afraid of her."

"Whites as well as blacks?"

"Perhaps. I don't know. Only Babalayou, the fetisher, was not afraid of her. He said he was going to kill her."

"You heard him say that?"

"Many people heard him say it."

"Because she took away Babalayou's dolls?"

"Ay-ee! How do you know such things?"

"Have you anything you would like to ask him, Prudence?"

"Yes. Who, my friend, is the most important woman in this town? The one whose ears are the biggest because everybody is always whispering into them?"

"There are several, mother. Perhaps the one who hears the most is Anoma. She was the senior wife of the old Sarkin, the chief. She is my grandmother's sister, sir. She should have been the queen mother now, but there was a big palaver over the succession to the stool and then her son, my uncle, was killed. Some said it was murder. So she is a woman who is always listening and what she hears she keeps as carefully as a farmer keeps his seed corn."

"Then I shall ask you to take me to see her. What is your name?"

"It is Yosofo, mother."

"Fine," said Quarshie, "we will send for you, Yosofo, when we need your help."

After the young man had gone Mrs. Quarshie said, "There will be much that was said, amongst the market women, about the woman who lived here. I sometimes wonder if there are amongst them witches who can travel without being seen and who conceal themselves in the roofs of people's huts so that they can hear what is being said."

Outside the windows of the rest house a brown-paper tree rustled its noisy leaves and the heat that surged through the closed shutters was like the clutching fingers of a man being burned up by fever.

It was midafternoon and both the Quarshies were stretched naked and side by side on the bed. They had bathed before lying down but already their skins shone again with sweat.

Quarshie had his eyes shut but Mrs. Quarshie knew, from long experience, that, along with a certain rigidity of attitude, this meant not that he was resting but that he was turning the full force of his concentration on the problems surrounding the death of Martha Solveig.

Mrs. Quarshie was not finding the picture of the woman that was emerging from their investigations a very attractive one. Before they lay down Quarshie had said, "Knowledge is power —that's an old axiom. When you have knowledge about people you have power over them. Martha made a speciality, I suspect, of that kind of power and she was intelligent enough to know that people hate you for having power over them."

Somewhere, deep inside herself, Mrs. Quarshie found a spark of anger against Martha. She seemed to have been a mischief-maker and now she and Quarshie had been drawn into the turmoil the woman had left in her wake and she felt like advising Quarshie to give up the case and would have done so had she not known that it would be useless. Once he got a grip on any-thing it would, she knew, be necessary to cut off his hands be-fore he would let go. It was one of the reasons why he was so good at whatever he did, whether it was medicine, wood carv-ing or tracking down killers. It was also, curiously, in contrast to the other side of his character, his gentleness.

He interrupted her meditation by sitting up suddenly and saying irritably, "We are wasting time lying here when there is so much more that we need to know. Let's go down to the hospital and see if we can find Levitsky or the young American couple."

Outside, the air carried a force of heat that struck from every side. As they drove through the town Mrs. Quarshie thought it looked as if a firing squad had passed along the street leaving every bit of shade strewn with corpses.

Quarshie, as sometimes happened, tuned in on the wave length of Mrs. Quarshie's thoughts and said, "Too pooped to pant. That's what they used to say in Canada. Though I suspect that a little later in the year the thermometer will notch up a few more degrees before the weather breaks."

When the Quarshies walked in on Terri and her husband, Trenton Smith, in the quarters they were occupying right beside the hospital, it was to find that they had not taken up the siesta habit but were sitting as far back as they could in the shadows of the deep verandah that fronted their bungalow and wearing as few clothes as possible. In Terri's case this meant a loose tunic-length gauze covering for the upper part of her body and a tiny bikini-style *cache-sex*. Trenton was wearing abbreviated swimming trunks.

Both of them had modified Afro hair styles, light skin and were very tall and willowy. Terri had very arresting grey eyes. To Mrs. Quarshie they looked more like brother and sister than husband and wife.

Quarshie said, "Forgive me for barging in like this, in this heat and at this time of day, but Colonel Jedawi, the President, has sent me up here to investigate the death of Miss Solveig, and I would like to ask you a few questions. I shall, of course, very much appreciate any help you can give us. I am Dr. Quarshie and this is my wife."

The Smiths were obviously startled and Trenton got to his feet with some alacrity.

"Why, Doctor," he said, "we weren't expecting you . . .

leastways, not yet. Of course Ephraim told us you were going to be working on the case. And we heard that you had arrived this morning . . . but you certainly move fast, don't you? You are welcome, nonetheless, though I'm afraid that in this heat our brains may not work too well—I guess they get baked hard and then crumble. Please sit down. Mrs. Quarshie, why don't you share this seat with my wife, Terri. My name is Trenton. Now . . . the legend reached us, Doctor, that you are in the habit of drinking beer, so may I offer you a bottle?"

"You are very kind," said Quarshie. "Will you be drinking too?"

"Drinking beer with the famous Dr. Quarshie is something I will be able to tell my children about. Will you drink beer as well, Mrs. Quarshie? The only other thing I can offer is cold water."

"Which will do me very nicely," said Mrs. Quarshie.

While Trenton went to fetch the drinks and Quarshie lowered himself rather gingerly into a somewhat fragile-looking cane chair Mrs. Quarshie turned to Terri and asked, "And how are you managing with our climate, Mrs. Smith? Do you ever have anything like it in America?"

"Not where I come from. It does get hot in New York in the summer and all that glass and concrete reflects the heat back so that it can be pretty bad, but it never gets as hot as it gets here. It's probably around a hundred twelve, a hundred fifteen degrees right now. That's awfully hot."

"And how do you get along with the people?" Quarshie asked.

"To us of course it's another world. We expected it to be different, but not like this."

"In what do you find the greatest difference?"

Terri thought a moment and then replied slowly, "I guess it has got to do with integrity, in the true sense of the word—you know, everything being a part of everything else. Wholeness. I mean all the pieces of people's lives fit together, though, of course, those pieces are nothing like as complicated as the lives of people back home. In our society it's like everyone is given a great big jig-saw puzzle, which would be O.K. if only all the pieces belonged to the picture you are supposed to be making up. Discontinuity, I guess that's another word that says what I mean. The people here don't even really have a past, a present and a future. They think and act as if it is all one."

"Is that something you like or dislike?"

"I think it's wonderful, I really do."

Trenton came back with the drinks. "What's wonderful?" he asked.

"The people we have to deal with in our clinics out here."

"You can say that again. You know, Doctor, I get a different feeling about the meaning of the word 'primitive' every time I have dealings with them. It makes our habit of thinking about our way of life as being advanced kind of sick. I guess that's why we don't make it with brother Ephraim. He's trying all the time to push people around here into 'advanced' patterns. And as for Martha . . . I reckon you really came to talk about her . . . man, we met head-on. She was a typical paternalist and proof that the female of the species is deadlier than the male."

"Then you don't disapprove of the people here the way so many Afro-Americans I have met do? You don't get thrown by the way they see things and do things?"

"Oh, sure we get thrown, but not in the direction we expected to get thrown. Of course I understand Ephraim's problems. He is right where the crunch is." Trenton poured beer for himself and for Quarshie. "Once, when I was doing some postgraduate work in psychology, I was sent to make a report on the people working in a General Motors plant. The idea was to sort out, psychologically speaking, the lame ducks. And do you know what I found? Stress was the thing I had to measure. Well, the management people all talked about the rat race and the pressures, and the people on the production line were pathologically bored. But both those groups were being, or felt they were being, more or less adequately rewarded for what they were doing. No, the men who really took the beating were shop foremen. They were in the middle. They got pushed by management and sworn at, all the time, by the men on the floor whom they had to push. That's where Ephraim is at. He's got the army and the technocrats leaning on him on one side, and on the other side he has to spend his time hacking at all his people's roots. Like I said, we don't get along all that well, but we can understand some of his problems."

"Did you know about his relationship with Martha?"

"Who didn't? That was something else which made our acquaintance with him difficult. She was using him, like she used everyone. If I said that she got what she had coming to her you'd think that I'm a real son of a bitch. But really . . . she had one great talent and it was to make trouble for everyone. She was pushy. Aggressive."

"Yet I hear that she had some kind of sympathetic relationship with Mrs. Levitsky."

"So you are onto that one already? You want to comment, Terri?"

"You know what she made me think of in that situation?" Terri said. "A tigress stalking a kill, all soft patty paws and purrs. There was maybe a sex thing going there as well, which Martha was exploiting. They were two women full of their own conflicts. Poor Mrs. Levitsky has been screwed every which way by life, and Martha was great at screwing herself. And then, Martha had a professional interest in the hunt."

"She was after a story?"

Terri nodded. "One that will come to the surface, so I am told, tomorrow."

"Really?"

"It may only be hearsay. But Martha was always digging at everyone. She even tried us. She wanted to do an interview with us on how we sophisticated folk reacted to the land of our ancestors."

Trenton said, "Oh, she was a grade-A bitch, I can tell you. When we told her how we reacted, you know, like primitive Africa was more civilised than the uncivilised West, she got as pissed as hell . . . and I can tell you this heat did not help. . . . We got down to name-calling, the works. Some of the hospital staff heard us at it and came and stood around outside. I guess they'd never seen anything like it before. When she left she slammed the screen door so hard it came off the top hinge."

"So you didn't love her?"

"Not at all, Doctor, not at all."

"Who else didn't love her?"

"You mean who else might want to kill her?" Trenton examined the thought before he answered his own question. "I could have done it, I guess. But I didn't. I would think the answer would be one man, René something or other. They made a good couple. He's a type that is overdue for extinction, too. He's a . . . how do they say it, *'le vieux colonial'* . . . the old colonial. All blacks to them are some kind of subspecies. Or, at their best, children."

Terri said, "They were about the same age, too. And they as thick as thieves, though I don't know what it was they were up to. And, Doctor, don't take too much notice of what we are saying because most of it relates to feelings rather than facts."

"What about Dr. Levitsky? Do you think he might have been reacting badly to the tigress hunting his wife?"

"He's beautiful." It was Terri's comment. "Everybody thinks so. He would never react destructively to anyone. No, I mean it. He's good and totally unselfish. I've never met anyone like him before."

"I'll go along with that." Trenton endorsed his wife's statement. "There is no one else here who is worth a square millimeter off the skin of Levitsky's left foot."

Looking at her husband, Mrs. Quarshie felt that she might have said the same of him.

"So who else do you want to know about? You know it's wonderful to get all this off our chests and do it for a good reason. Levitsky is the only one we can really talk to but he has too much on his plate already. However, I can tell you this place has been buzzing since Ephraim has been around telling everyone you were on your way up here and what a reputation you have."

Quarshie said, "The reputation I have has about as much

truth in it as the sands of the desert up north have water. It does have its values, though. For instance, since my imminent arrival was announced have you noticed anyone walking around looking nervous, or upset?"

Trenton laughed. "For all anyone shows anything here they might all be a bunch of snakes. You know, no face muscles. Though the old man, Percy, might have been a little more animated than usual, wouldn't you say, Terri?"

"He's kind of cute, too," was his wife's response. "Playing the courtly old gentleman all the time. He's like an antique, he has that beautiful gloss you find on polished old wood."

"What makes you say that, um, Percy has been more animated?"

"Just that I've seen him around a lot more. Most of the time he stays home, plays Bach cantatas on a contraption he has in his garden which he rigged up himself, and reads up on local history. He still writes papers for international historical societies. I can tell you he's a real original."

"And still kind of cute?"

Quarshie poured himself another glass of beer, looked at it thoughtfully and then said, "Since I am investigating Martha's death there is one question I have to ask everyone who had any connection with her."

"Yeah, yeah, I know," said Trenton. "Where were you on the night of . . . let me see what was it? December the twentieth." He thought for a moment and then said, "I guess we weren't too far away from the scene of the crime. You see, we have a clinic up north near the frontier post and the day she appears to have died was our day for visiting that clinic. I treat the children while Terri does her nutrition research. The clinic closed late, as it usually does, but that doesn't worry us. The foundation provided us with our own truck and we have mosquito netting around the back so that we can sleep in it and we carry a camping stove and food and water. You know the nights up here are right out of this world. Stars as close to each other in the sky as sequins on a torch singer's evening gown. Silence that makes you afraid to speak out loud. And space.

Man, you get the feeling that you just have to be the first people who ever walked around out there. It all gives time a different dimension."

Looking at the young Americans, Quarshie began to feel a liking for them. Their slave ancestors, he thought, might have come from the desert regions of the Eastern Sudan, maybe Nuers or Dinkas, and the feeling Trenton had shown for the empty spaces of Africa might have been in his genes. Though the genetic inheritance would have been modified by the sperm of some white man or other. Strange that out of five percent of all the slaves who were shipped out of Africa and wound up in America two of them should have "come home" to an area that was not unlike the one from which their ancestors had probably been stolen. Quarshie almost remarked on it but another question came to his mind.

"What about the other white up here? The contractor, or builder or whatever he is."

Terri said, "I hadn't been here three days before he made a pass at me. Since then I've kept away from him."

"We've both kept away from him," Trenton told Quarshie. "I know that he's a rich man and that he spends a lot of his money on black women. The talk in the market is that he keeps a harem of them. We pass him quite often on our way to and from our clinics, which are dotted around the countryside. A lot of the time he's out supervising construction work, fixing bridges after they get washed out by flash floods and things like that. Once, when Terri wasn't with me, he stopped and invited me to have a beer with him. He travels in a kind of caravan which has everything, air conditioning, refrigerator, double bed and pictures of African women all over the place." Trenton shook his head. "In my book he doesn't know anything about how to win friends and influence people."

Quarshie put down his empty glass. "You've been a lot of help," he said. "And I expect we shall be seeing much more of you. But if we're to catch Dr. Levitsky before he goes home, we had better be on our way." He got up, and then, as he went down the steps of the verandah, he said, "Oh, one more question. When you go for your little jaunts in your truck do you stay by the roadside, or do you go off into the bush?"

"Depending on the condition of the ground, we go off a mile or two if we can. We feel more at liberty to do whatever we feel like doing then."

Quarshie nodded and said, "I see." But what he saw was not at all clear to him, though it left Trenton, as he hoped it would, with a slightly uneasy feeling that he had either said too much, or too little.

CHAPTER FOUR

"She looked like the victim of a tiger out hunting in red weather."

The Quarshies had only just gotten over the formalities of introducing themselves to Dr. Levitsky and were seated facing him across his desk in his consulting room at the hospital when his telephone rang.

The heat of the afternoon was subsiding a little and the doctor had an electric fan which distributed its benison over an arc of about sixty degrees. A puff of hot air, therefore, reached Mrs. Quarshie every twenty seconds or so, and it helped, in a small way, to dry the sweat on her face, her neck and her plump bare arms.

As she watched the doctor answer his call she thought there was something embryonic about his appearance, a wise embryo with a dome-like forehead over a thick line of almost straight, black, bushy eyebrows. Beneath the eyebrows were very deep-set eyes like lights at the end of a tunnel, but very bright and enquiring. His nose was not very significant but below it there was a thick, black-tinged-with-grey moustache which was cut straight above his upper lip and supported by exceptionally deep curving lines that bracketed his mouth.

The clearest statement his looks made about him was to proclaim that he was male but it was something which did not carry over into his voice, which was soft and almost pale where his looks were harsh and dark.

He said gently, after acknowledging that the caller was speaking to Dr. Levitsky and then listening, without interruption, for a long time, "You have done all the right things. I am glad you were there. Don't move her again. Build some shade around her and keep people away from her . . . even her relatives. Can you do that?" There was a pause. "Well, do your best. I know it will be difficult. I am leaving at once. I will be there"—he glanced at his watch—"in an hour." Pause. "Yes.

You can give her ten milligrams of morphine, intramuscular. Right?" Pause. "Yes. You are a good man. I'm coming."

He hung up. For a moment he looked reflectively at the Quarshies. Then he asked, "You are a nurse, aren't you, Mrs. Quarshie?"

"A nurse midwife."

"Better still. That was one of my dispensers calling from Togbe, a little town about thirty miles away. A pregnant woman was knocked down on the road. It sounds as if she is badly injured. Do you want to come with me, both of you? My staff, here, are overworked. We'll give them a bit of a holiday. You drive, of course, Dr. Quarshie?" And when Quarshie nodded, Levitsky went on. "Then we can take my pickup. It has a bed in the back and we will go and see what we can do for the woman and perhaps bring her into the hospital. We shall be able to talk."

Quarshie was already on his feet.

Levitsky sat squashed between Mrs. Quarshie and her husband, who was behind the steering wheel. The big man was driving fast, but not recklessly. It was the nature of driving in Africa that he "horned," as they say, frequently. Sheep, goats, chickens, dogs and most people treated the road as if it had been built for their use and pleasure rather than for wheeled traffic. Though the road was blacktop, sand drifted across it like wind-driven snowdrifts across highways and it seemed as if every vehicle was towing its own dust storm; the red soil soon mixed with the sweat of the people and streaked their faces terra cotta.

Levitsky said, in his soft voice, following a question from Quarshie, "Oh, I have pushed a lot of rocks up a lot of mountains, Doctor, which makes me one of the natural descendants of Sisyphus. If you asked me to summarise my philosophy in a few words I would quote Camus. He said, 'Perhaps we cannot prevent this world from being a world in which children are tortured. But we can reduce the number of tortured children.' I would change that only to the extent of saying not that we 'can,' but that we 'must.'"

"What rocks would you say you have pushed up the mountain, Doctor?"

Levitsky closed his eyes as a cloud of squawking chickens filled the air in front of the truck. "Being born a Jew was a good one to start with because I don't like being a Jew. I don't like being categorized. I like to be just a man amongst other men. I grew up near the Mile End Road in London. Jews were thicker around there than they are in Tel Aviv today. Or so it seemed because they stuck out like fat men always do in the company of the thin. My father came from Poland and he was in what is called 'the rag trade,' using sweated labour to make cheap clothes. He made a lot of money, too, and I didn't like him although he was never cruel to me. My mother, in fact, pushed him into spending most of the money which he had wrung out of other people on me. I got the best education that was available. But the cockneys called us 'kikes' and I didn't blame them for it. That was a rock," he said with feeling, "to have been born a Jew. Of course, they are a clever people. There are more geniuses amongst them than in any other race. And then in every society in which they live, they have a curious habit. When everybody else starts off on the right foot they start off on the left through sheer perversity."

Mrs. Quarshie heard the tune of Levitsky's statements without quite getting the words, but she sat still, listening.

Levitsky said, "It's nice to have someone to talk to who understands me." He was addressing Quarshie. "I can't say these things to anyone around here. But I know that you hear what I am saying, don't you?"

"I do."

"In some ways you are a bit like me, aren't you? It's something to do with our trade and at the same time it goes beyond it.

"We have to take the right fork here," Levitsky said. "And then it is only a couple of miles to Togbe."

The woman had been lying beside the road behind a matting screen. Her injuries were serious, but not mortal. Her right arm and her right leg were broken and there was an injury to her ribs on that side. But the main concern was the foetus. They were taking her back to the hospital now to check the baby's condition and to see whether there was a chance that she might bring it to term.

The back of the pickup had been roofed and given canvas side screens and Mrs. Quarshie was in there with the patient and her sister, who would cook for her and care for her while she was in hospital, a procedure often followed in small bush hospitals. The few trained nurses performed only tasks which required their skills like taking temperatures and changing dressings on wounds.

Quarshie was driving more slowly, trying to avoid the worst potholes and bumps in the road as these appeared in his headlights. It was an exercise that became increasingly difficult as his windshield became more and more spattered with the remains of large insects which virtually exploded on impact.

Both he and Levitsky were tired but he made a great effort to overcome this because he thought it might work to his advantage and that Levitsky might be somewhat more unguarded in his responses.

"Martha's murder must have been a terrible thing," he said tentatively.

"Yes. Though, strange as it may seem, I suspect that it may have been almost more terrible for the murderer. He must have lost all control and only awakened to what he had done later. She looked like the victim of a tiger out hunting in red weather. Though she must have invited it. I'm sorry to say that, but it's true. She was a danger to everyone."

Quarshie swerved to avoid a bump which was exaggerated by his headlights and nearly went off the road onto the very soft shoulder.

"What did she do specifically?" he asked when he had the truck safely back on course.

"It was not by doing so much as being. Her potentialities were the threat."

"Even to you?"

"Particularly to me."

"Why?"

"To my wife. You have not met her. You will get the answer to your question tomorrow. You are coming to our Christmas party, aren't you? I told Ephraim to tell you you were invited."

"Thank you, yes, we'd like to come." Otherwise, how else shall we get to know this mystery woman? Quarshie stored the question in his mind without voicing it.

"You don't want to tell me what kind of threat Martha was to your wife?" Quarshie asked after Levitsky had remained silent for quite a long time.

"No, not until after you've met her." He narrowed his eyes and considered what he was going to say before he told Quarshie, "But there was something else I think you should know about Martha. I got a different view of her one day. She came to see me at my surgery and for the first and only time I felt that she was unsure of herself. She was worried and she wanted to tell me something, but she could not seem to get around to it. At one point she said that her mission in life looked as if it was going to abort . . . that was the word she used. She said she had to tell someone. Then she backed off and started talking about the need for humanitarian principles in the world and that she was not really a bad woman. After that she shut up."

Quarshie was conscious that Levitsky had turned in his seat and was staring at his profile as if he was wondering what kind of a man he was and how much, perhaps, he could confide in him. If that was true Levitsky evidently came to the conclusion that he had gone as far as he could, because, after a couple of moments, he said, "In the end, she told me she would go away and think through her problem herself and come back and talk to me about it afterwards. That was about three weeks before she died and she never did mention the subject again. But the last time I met her I got the feeling that if she had lost her confidence when she came to see me, she had regained it and was back to being her normal, aggressive self. I am sorry I can't be more helpful."

As is usual in the Sahelian regions at that time of year, the temperature dropped rapidly with nightfall from around a hundred-plus degrees to almost half that and it was something neither Quarshie nor his wife were accustomed to. In Port St. Mary it tended to be fairly hot and sticky most of the time.

Once they got back to the hospital they helped Levitsky in the operating theatre, where their patient's broken limbs were put in plaster, and having determined that the foetus was dead, it was Quarshie who removed it by Caesarean section, and then, at last, the Quarshies went back to the rest house to bathe again, for the third time since their arrival at midday, and to get into bed.

Both of them were overtired, which meant that their minds spun on unchecked though they were physically exhausted.

Quarshie, flat on his back, said, "Did you get the last thing Levitsky said before we left?"

"No, I was already in the car."

"He said, 'Merry Christmas.' I don't understand it. I don't believe he knew what he was saying."

"I thought he was very nice the way he thanked me for our help," Mrs. Quarshie said. "He thinks you are wonderful. He said you have a marvellous pair of hands and that if you had not been here he would probably have made a mess of the Caesarean because he was so tired."

Quarshie thought about that before he said, "He was testing me. The way he worked on those fractures did not suggest that he was exceptionally tired. If she is reasonably lucky that woman won't have anything to show that she was as smashed up as she was."

"Don't you think he is a good man?"

Quarshie lay with his eyes shut. Something troubled him apart from his wife's love of clear distinctions about whether people were good or bad. Presently he replied, "I don't know. When I used to box the coach used to say, 'Watch your footwork. It can keep you out of trouble better than anything you can do with your hands.' I have a feeling that perhaps it's a lesson Levitsky has learned as well. I don't know. My feelings have been wrong before. Your intuition says he is O.K., eh?"

"I can't see how anyone could feel otherwise."

Quarshie grunted, sensing that a curtain was, at last, coming down on a very long day and that he should not fight that feeling. "Time will tell," he said, "time will tell." And then, turning his head and looking at the soft curves of Mrs. Quarshie's body, he said, "I'm a lucky man. At the end of the day I only have to look at you to know what pleasures there are in store for me. It's like seeing a ripe mango on a tree and knowing that"—he yawned hugely—"it will still be there tomorrow waiting to be picked." And he reached out and ran his hand down the curve of her hip and fell gently off the edge of a tiresomely confused world into sleep.

CHAPTER FIVE

"We die because we have invented death."

The heat returned in the morning burning with the same or even greater force than it had the day before. It was relentless.

Quarshie reminded himself that it was Christmas Day and he remembered how he had watched people in Canada celebrate with Christmas trees bedecked with coloured lights standing in the snow outside their homes. He was not mission-trained, as were so many others who left Africa for their education overseas, and the bonhomie he had seen everywhere around Montreal had appeared to him to be a charade which everyone had seemed to be bent on playing out.

Like Dr. Levitsky, people had said, "Merry Christmas," and he supposed that in a way they had meant it but . . . the impulse behind it seemed to have been a conditioned reflex.

In contrast to the Canadian snows, here, though it was only half-past nine, the sun was already the fierce enemy of everything which moved except the tree lizards and the snakes. Beyond the scalloped edge of the corrugated asbestos roof of the bungalow the vista was filled with a dazzling ferocity of light and deep shadows with no gradations of darkness between them.

There was not even any wind, so the brown-paper tree was silent.

Somewhere a kite shrilled and Quarshie wondered why. Was it to indicate rapacity, hunger, triumph because, perhaps, it had seen some sort of prey or offal from which it could make a meal, or was it merely announcing its claim to the territory over which it hunted?

It had probably been to foil kites and vultures that someone had buried Martha's body under a cairn of stones and Quarshie again wondered why anyone had gone to all that trouble. Why not leave the body to be picked to the bone by scavengers? When anyone committed murder his instinct would surely be to try to conceal the corpus delicti? A body, even a decomposing one, was much easier to identify than the few bones that would be left after the carrion eaters had done their work.

"We die because we have invented death." Somewhere he had read those words and they came back to him now as he sat looking over the rocky landscape through half-closed eyes. To animals death has none of the importance that men give it. Certainly some instinct for preservation informed them that it was something which had to be avoided. However, when they came upon the bodies of others of their species, they either ignored them or, if they were meat eaters, they fed off them.

Only men had given all kinds of importance to dying instead of treating it as the inevitable end to all physical substance and therefore an integral part of an endless process.

So, had the murderer been overcome by an excess of human sentimentality after, as Levitsky had said, behaving like "a tiger in red weather"?

It was a thought which threw some kind of light on the character of the man who had killed Martha, whatever the answer to that question might be.

Quarshie's Christmas meditation had been prompted by the fact that he had nothing else to do. Mrs. Quarshie was still inside asleep and he did not want to awaken her.

There were still three white expatriates—four including Mrs. Levitsky, Hanna, whom he had yet to see. He could not, however, burst in on any of them on this sanctified morning and ask them what they had been doing on the day when Martha Solveig was murdered. There was also the fetish priest, whom he would have to question.

Dr. Levitsky's post-mortem had established that Martha had been dead for less than forty-eight hours when they brought her body in. It had also established that she had been killed by a heavy blow on the back of the head which had smashed the occipital region of the skull. It was a blow, Levitsky had said, which suggested to him that it might have been delivered while she was bending forward. It was his opinion that it was after she had been killed by that blow that she was stoned. In his own words, "It was as if someone had lost his mind in his fury and had pelted her inanimate body with rocks." But, when Quarshie asked him for the evidence on which he had based that assumption he had admitted, quite simply, that he had none. "It was a conclusion I came to when I thought about it afterwards and tried to imagine the scene. Could you, for instance, see her running around while someone chased her throwing stones at her? Nor were there any marks on her wrists or ankles to suggest that she had been tied up."

"Did you and Ephraim go back along the trail that she left when she had been dragged?"

"No, we were out there at about midday, you know? There is not a scrap of shade anywhere and the rocks were so hot they were burning my feet through the soles of my shoes. Besides we were both in something of a state of shock. We just got her onto the stretcher and then walked back the two miles to the road. She was very heavy and the two policemen who were carrying her kept having to put her down to take a rest. It was all very distasteful and unpleasant. Poor Martha. Even in death she was a prime nuisance."

"Did Ephraim seem very upset?" Quarshie had asked.

"We were both very upset. I'm not squeamish. I deal with several nasty road accidents a week here. But somehow they are natural occurrences these days. What we were faced with out there was grotesque."

It was something which seemed to be true of the whole case, Quarshie thought. And it seemed as if there were more bizarre things to come from the way everyone kept talking about Dr. Levitsky's Christmas party.

He decided, on an impulse, to wake Mrs. Quarshie anyway. When he went in, however, he found that she was lying on her back with her eyes open. Wordlessly, he stood looking down on her from the end of the bed until she, also wordlessly, raised her arms to him and he accepted her invitation.

"I came up here all alone because my husband had preceded me by a couple of months," Hanna Levitsky told Quarshie. She had already told him that she was Polish by birth and when she spoke her "W's" turned into "V's" and she had a little trouble with her prepositions. "It was my first taste of Africa. And it was the top of the storm season. In that time the thunder takes you and shakes you, so huge it is. I thought every day I am going to die. The bridge to the main road was washed completely away. Shirley was there to meet me when I arrived. There are three sections and only one single plank from one pier to the next. It was nearly midnight. An African was walking in front of me over the planks carrying a hurricane lamp. Shirley walked behind holding me by the belt. Underneath I could see nothing, only darkness."

Quarshie glanced away from his hostess across the wide, roofless, circular verandah to look at Shirley. He was very dapper, dressed in a cream-coloured linen suit with short sleeves and a shirt collar that was designed to be worn open. In profile he had an impressive head, one that might have belonged to a diplomat. His greying hair was neatly cut and well brushed and he had an ascetic look which was not at all associated in Quarshie's mind with what Trenton had told him of the man. There was, however, one factor which was out of kilter with the rest of his appearance: his forearms were not only unusually muscular, they were also heavily tattooed.

"It must have been a terrifying experience," Quarshie said, returning his attention to Hanna Levitsky.

"It was, it was. But that was not all, Doctor." She told him, "When we got here, Sol, my husband, was outside in the bush somewhere patching a man who was mauled by a lion. So the man who met me here on this spot was the D.O., not Ephraim but the one which was in front from him. Today, I like this verandah, especially at night when the roof is made from stars. But that night with lightning and thunder everywhere it was like a platform in hell. It is so high up, no? When there is a little wind it receives it all. Often we sleep out here at night. Of course, it is dangerous for the children, but you cannot have everything all at the same time."

Quarshie was about to exclaim that he had not heard anything about the Levitskys having any children but there was no interrupting her—the story she was telling possessed her. "The D.O., he was such a nice young man, very polished and polite, took me inside. There was a lamp like this one burning in there, in the big room. I shall never forget it. It was strange, weird . . . and I was not listening to what the D.O. was saying until I heard him telling me, 'Your husband's predecessor hung himself from that beam in the middle from the ceiling. Poor man, he went mad.'" Hanna Levitsky laughed mirthlessly. "Oh dear," she said, "I thought I was going to fall to pieces at the spot, like dust and dry sticks. It was all too much after that long drive and the thunder and the bridge and everything." Her face was flushed with the emotion she had been reliving. Then she drew back and returned behind her defences, concluding, simply, "But I like it now. It is my home, our home. Sol's and mine."

Her blue eyes were slightly hyperthyroid and a movement at the head of the long flight of steps which led to the ground level below caught her attention. "Now, at last, there's Percy. I must go and have a word with him. I'm afraid that if he sees the Christmas tree inside he may give away the game before we are ready for it." She got up from the canvas chair she had been sitting in and went to meet her new guest.

Percy was very tall and thin and he wore a high, starched collar around a neck that was as stringy as a turkey's.

Quarshie took a long pull at his beer.

To his right, on a high pedestal, the pressure lamp hissed, giving a brilliant light which bleached the colour out of everything, particularly Hanna Levitsky's dress. It was a daffodil yellow, very simple and cool-looking, especially as she did not appear to be wearing anything underneath it. Beside Percy she seemed to be even tinier than she was in reality, though her rump and thighs were surprisingly well fleshed. She was wearing her almost waist-length red hair tied back with a wide pale-blue ribbon.

The night, as usual on the fringes of the Sahara at this season, had brought a surcease to the heat of the day. And the stars, as Hanna Levitsky had pointed out, hung in their millions overhead; closer to each other than the lights of Manhattan as Quarshie had seen them from the Staten Island Ferry in New York.

The children Hanna Levitsky had mentioned were still surprisingly quiet.

There was a wreath hung over the door that she had said led into the big room and there was a red candle flickering in the window beside the door.

Hanna Levitsky, Quarshie thought, was almost like a child herself, petite, ethereal and showing few signs of her age, though she must have been over fifty.

Ephraim, who had collected them at the rest house, had talked a little bit more about her on the way to the party. "The story is, as I told you, that the doctor picked her up right out of a German concentration camp. All her relatives had been killed and she was very young. Even now he treats her more as if she were his daughter than his wife. She still has a number tattooed on her wrist and she never covers it with a bracelet, or long sleeves."

Looking at her again, Quarshie saw that, aside from her wide hips, her other bones looked as fragile and tiny as those of a small bird and he thought of her, perhaps in her teens, being brutalised by savage men.

Levitsky, carrying a guitar, came over and sat down next to Quarshie in the chair Hanna had just vacated.

"Quite a menagerie, eh?" he asked Quarshie as he settled himself. "I have been watching you looking around. Now that Percy has arrived we can start our regular program for the evening and I am the first act." He tapped his guitar lightly and said, "Next to Hanna this is my greatest love. I learned to play it in another desert, in Libya, when I was attached to a Polish brigade during Hitler's war. It has become quite a passion. I hope you are not too knowledgeable about music."

Quarshie almost said that he did not know the first thing about it and then restrained himself as Levitsky began to play.

Over the opening chords, as he picked them from his instrument, he said, "This is a Portuguese fado." It was a melancholy piece of music, full of a kind of sadness that was foreign to Quarshie's African soul.

In a moment or two Levitsky's song and his guitar were the only sounds to be heard and Quarshie was suddenly conscious that below the verandah, on the ground, there was a crowd of people from the town who had come to listen and were as still and silent as the elite above them.

Despite the fact that it was foreign, the sadness of the song appeared to reach everyone even though no one understood the words.

As he sang Levitsky was transformed and became a different man who spoke to people through other senses than those they used in their everyday involvement with survival. Even his voice took on a different dimension and became a surprisingly resonant baritone.

When he finished everyone on the verandah and those below it applauded.

Percy said, as the applause died down, "Sing 'In der Ferne,' Sol."

Levitsky closed his eyes and played a few chords, then he stopped and shook his head. "I don't think I can do it," he said.

His wife said, "Please, Sol. We want to hear it. It's Christmas."

Levitsky took a deep breath and started again. This time he did not stop.

He was singing in German and Quarshie doubted whether any of those around him, except perhaps Percy, knew the language. Yet all of them, he was sure, would feel the pain of the song. His singing was heavy with regret and, Quarshie thought, nostalgia, or remembrance untainted by mawkishness.

After he finished Levitsky looked up with a challenge in his eye as if he defied anyone to make fun of the feeling with which he had sung.

Shirley said, "Christ, Sol . . . you'll 'ave me crying in me beer. What does it mean?"

"Schmaltz. It's about homesickness, I suppose. It says, unhappy are those who wander about the world, who forget their homelands and the place of their birth. And . . . no, I can't translate it."

"You don't need to," Quarshie said.

Levitsky said, "Schubert," as if that explained everything, and started playing a piece which was all runs and clever fingering.

It did not demand Quarshie's attention and he looked around the circle of people sitting on the verandah. There were René Dupré, Trenton and Terri Smith, with Mrs. Quarshie between them, Ephraim, Mrs. Levitsky, Percy, Shirley, Levitsky and himself. Who was there amongst them, he wondered, who knew more about Martha's death than was healthy for them, or more than they had told him?

For the first time he looked closely at the Frenchman, Dupré.

It was easy to recognise what Martha had seen in him that appealed to her. He had the look of what Quarshie had heard spoken of as the Latin lover, and along with his darkly handsome, though aging, features there was more than a tincture of dissolution. In fact, Quarshie suspected that Monsieur Dupré's veins contained a fair percentage of Arab blood. That the man was the same one whom the French ambassador had asked him to look out for seemed to be at least possible, if not probable. Which made him a man with a well-established criminal record who would, undoubtedly, be up to some kind of mischief.

Levitsky said, "Now a little Polish folk music. And then we come to the big moment, the big scene." There was something in Levitsky's tone of voice which made Quarshie examine his expression very carefully. Levitsky caught the look and said, "I have to go through with it, please understand that. Think of it as . . . as therapy."

He played several more tunes, ending with one which Quarshie recognised as a carol that is sung all over the world about good King Wenceslaus. When it was over Hanna Levitsky walked to the door and, standing under the wreath, turned and faced the verandah and told everyone:

"Come in, now, all of you. It's time we had the Christmas tree."

Then, when she had them settled in the big circle around the extravagantly decorated tree with real candles on it, she left the room by a side door.

Levitsky still had his guitar but was playing it very softly, a small tinkling piece which made the instrument sound like a muffled music box.

Quarshie wanted to hold his breath and, then, to break his feeling of tension. He turned to Ephraim, who was sitting beside him, with the intention of making a comment about the fire hazard posed by the obviously very dry Christmas tree but Ephraim did not pay any attention to him when he spoke his name. Instead he stared fixedly at an open doorway to the left of the tree.

Hanna Levitsky was standing just inside the room, her arms slightly outstretched on each side of her, holding her hands as people sometimes do when they are about to dive into a pool.

She looked around the room at her guests, then down to the empty floor on each side of her, and said, "Here they are— Marja and Mishka. Run along, darlings, and say hullo to kind Uncle Percy, who brought you those lovely presents under the tree." And she threw her hands forward a little as if she were urging her two children towards the old man.

Quarshie found that now he really was holding his breath and his eyes were riveted on Hanna Levitsky's serene face.

Percy said, speaking to the air, just in front of his knees, "Merry Christmas, my dears. My goodness how you have grown." And to Hanna: "They are much less shy than they were last year."

Hanna replied, "They always have to come to you, first, don't they, Percy? They love you very much and remember you every night in their prayers."

Levitsky had stopped playing his guitar and the only sound

in the room was the chirruping of a cricket somewhere in a corner.

"Perhaps you would go to the nice African lady, children, and wish her a happy Christmas."

She was speaking of Mrs. Quarshie, and her husband felt a kind of rigor mortis creeping through his muscles.

Mrs. Quarshie was childless, too, and in African society that was as much of a handicap as being born with some kind of deformity.

He did not dare to turn his head but looked at her out of the corners of his eyes.

He need not have worried.

Though he knew that the wound from which Hanna Levitsky was suffering would be causing as much pain to Mrs. Quarshie, she did not show it.

She opened her arms and made a gesture which would have swept the two children to her, holding them on each side of her knees. Then, turning from one to the other she said, "What a pretty girl and what a handsome boy. Merry Christmas, both of you"—for a moment her voice broke and she paused to get it under control—"and . . . and I hope you get lots of beautiful presents."

Hanna Levitsky's voice, Quarshie thought he caught a note of something like relief in it, came right in saying, "Why don't you bring them to the tree, Mrs. Quarshie, so that they can see for themselves?"

With a strength of will Quarshie had seen his wife display on other crucial occasions Mrs. Quarshie got up and, holding out her hands, as Hanna Levitsky had done when she first appeared in the doorway, she led Marja and Mishka to the tree.

Then kneeling down and talking softly all the time, she opened all the presents and made two piles of them, one for Marja and the other for Mishka.

Levitsky started to play his guitar again and his music, though only Percy knew it and nodded approvingly, was an arrangement of a Chopin polonaise.

Presently Mrs. Quarshie got to her feet and stood with her

hands held out on each side of her, talking about the lovely tree to Marja and Mishka. Then something made her turn around.

Hanna Levitsky was standing close behind her, her face white, and she was crying silently, two parallel beads of tears falling down her cheeks.

This time Mrs. Quarshie's arms went around real flesh and blood and very gently she led her hostess away towards the door by which she had made her original entrance.

CHAPTER SIX

"The price of that kind of gold is too often measured in blood."

Quarshie changed his mental image of Percy from a Dickensian one to that of an old reptile, a big iguana. The old man's bald head sloped back from a low forehead and prominent brows, beneath which his dark eyes focused intense interest on anything which came to their attention in the same way that a burning glass turns light into heat. Also, like a lizard, his skin was horny, particularly on the gnarled hands with which he enclosed the projecting arms of the chair he was sitting in.

Again the word "bizarre" crept unbidden into Quarshie's mind. It could have been used to justify their experience at Dr. Levitsky's. Now, at Percy's, bizarre could also justifiably be used to describe their surroundings.

Percy was an eccentric, and the border line, Quarshie thought, between eccentricity and mental disturbance could not be defined with any accuracy. Was the man mad? Only, Quarshie decided, if most of the norms in the society into which Percy had been born could be accepted without question as sane and healthy. At the moment, it seemed to Quarshie, Western society was badly enough disturbed for there to be something seriously wrong with the norms, a circumstance which put eccentrics in a better light.

He, Mrs. Quarshie and Percy were sitting on a slightly raised round platform of concrete under a conical thatched roof. There were no walls, only wooden pillars supporting the roof, which had very wide eaves. The light was provided by three hissing pressure lamps outside the area covered by the thatch.

"They create heat, attract bugs and are a fire hazard under a grass roof . . . but I must have light," Percy said, explaining the disposition of the lights. And, he added, "I designed all the furniture myself and had it made locally. Chairs with seats for people with long thighs, chairs in which big men could sit without feeling nervous . . . that one, Doctor. Then, there is the item which makes me the talk of the neighbourhood. This." He pointed to a frame which was about eight feet wide and five feet high. It was the front of a device which looked to Quarshie like an enormously enlarged set of bellows from an old-fashioned plate camera. From its cavernous opening it stretched back in a series of concertina-like folds, diminishing in size until it fitted the front opening of an old, spring-driven phonograph.

"When you hear music come out of this, Doctor, it is like the sea. You can dive right into it and it encompasses you. Martha used to come up often and indulge herself. She had a lot of things wrong with her but she understood music and appreciated it. Which was fortunate—for her, I mean. Though, of course, she had other important reasons for her visits. You'll drink beer, Doctor?" A steward had appeared without being called, carrying two buckets of ice with bottles of beer imbedded in one and bottles of soft drinks in the other. Mrs. Quarshie took Dubonnet and soda. The steward poured a whiskey soda for Percy and put the bucket with the beer in it beside Quarshie, placing a bottle opener on a nearby side table.

Then he left again without a word being spoken.

"Your health, Doctor. Mrs. Quarshie."

Quarshie raised his glass and returned the salute wordlessly.

As he put his glass down, Percy said, "I think we all needed that. Though he never shows any signs of strain one shares Sol's agony all the way through events like this. Hanna lives in a world of total fantasy. It is impossible to tell most of the time whether she is really with us or not. It's strange. He treats her, in public at least, with the deference that people used to pay to young princesses who would, one day, become queens.

"Once, when Sol was away attending to an epidemic of some sort in one of the bigger villages, Hanna came to see me and sat in that same chair you are sitting in, Mrs. Quarshie. Now, I'm going to betray what one might think of as a confidence but, from the way you behaved this evening, I know that you have the sensitivity to appreciate the . . . the preciousness of what I have to tell you.

"Well, she drank rather more than was good for her and I

think the alcohol washed the fantasy away and she got down to rock bottom, the real truth. It was as if she pulled a scab off a wound and it bled again, though she looked at the blood objectively. No tears, no drama—just cold, dry statements of fact. She was in a German concentration camp, you know. Her mother was Jewish, perhaps a prostitute, I don't know. She was seventeen and in the camp the guards kept her in their quarters. In the evening, instead of playing darts, like they would have in a British mess, they played with Hanna. They bet on who could make her scream the loudest without drawing blood, or using any kind of weapon. They fed her quite well but she was forced to eat naked on her hands and knees without using her hands, out of a dog's dish. And, of course, they took their pleasures with her in a way which made every brutal occurrence a case of rape."

Mrs. Quarshie shuddered and said, "How tragic."

"Yes, Mrs. Quarshie. There is that element in all men because almost always they're ready to take advantage of the weak."

"Would you say that Martha was weak?" Quarshie asked.

"No. Not in any sense. She would always be the exploiter, not the exploited. Such people quite often come to a violent end."

"And what, sir, was the true purpose of her visits to you?"

"Information. She wanted a lot of information."

"About gold?"

"How clever of you. How did you know that?"

Quarshie explained about the books. He said nothing about the three golden medallions he still had in his coat pocket.

He concluded by asking, "Did you go up to the house after you heard she was dead?"

The old man smiled. "To ask that question you probably know that I did. Though, at the time, I did not know about her murder. She had a paper I had written about Mansa Musa, the grandson of Sundiata. I wanted to collect it."

"And did you?"

"All her papers had been taken away."

"What time of the day was that?"

"About two o'clock, I think."

"Was there any specific aspect of the Malian trade in gold that interested her?"

"There was. I don't know how good your knowledge is of the history of the period."

"It is very slight."

"Well it was the time of the early Middle Ages in Europe and Mali had become the centre of the Mandingo Empire, which covered an area that, in Europe, would have extended from the present Russian frontier to the Atlantic and from the North Sea to the Mediterranean. Timbuktu, which was one of the most important towns in ancient Mali, was founded in the twelfth century and a university was started there at about the same date the English were setting up one at Cambridge. Also, at the same time that the English were building Canterbury Cathedral, Mansa Musa was building great brick mosques at Gao and Timbuktu.

"As for wealth, the greatest Mandingo king, Mansa Musa, made a pilgrimage to Mecca and took along with him five hundred slaves, each carrying a golden staff weighing three hundred pounds. In fact, he caused great embarrassment when he got to Cairo because, as an Egyptian chronicler, Allah al Omari, says, the gold in Egypt had enjoyed a high rate of exchange up to the moment Musa arrived. At that time a gold *mitgal* was worth twenty-five drachma. For twelve years thereafter the market was so flooded with gold that the *mitgal* never got above twenty-two drachma.

"Many Arab travellers visited Mali and left records of what they saw. One of them wrote, 'This Negro Lord is called Musa Mali, Lord of all the Negroes of Guinea. So abundant is the gold which is found in his country that he is the richest and most noble king in all the world.' Another said, 'The authority of Mali became mighty. All the nations of the Sudan stand in awe of it and the merchants of North Africa all travelled to that country.' Al Bakri, the most well known of these Arab authorities, wrote, later, that the people of Mali 'had a greater abhorrence of injustice than any other people' and that, 'neither the man who travelled nor he who stayed at home had anything to fear from robbers or from men of violence.'

"I am telling you all this to underline the fact that we are not talking about legends. This is no Prester John, but historical fact about one of the several great empires which existed here over a six-hundred-year period between 800 and about 1400 A.D.

"Such facts, however, were only of passing interest to Martha. As you rightly said, what really interested her was gold. She was particularly interested in a story that one of Mansa Musa's caravans got caught, with all its gold, in a freak sandstorm which lasted for months. The story says that the whole thing, beasts and men, were buried under the sand after they had died from the lack of water and food. She spent a lot of time amongst my books looking for any evidence that the story might have been true."

"Is it?"

"That is a question I would very much like to be able to answer myself. I don't know. Rumours still persist."

"Besides her dedication to the pursuit of gold was there any other aspect of Martha's character which was exceptional? You said she had a lot of things wrong with her."

"I am old-fashioned, Doctor, I freely admit it. And I say that to preface the statement that she boasted of being what she called a dyed-in-the-wool women's libber. She was always setting herself up in competition to men. It did not seem to me that she wanted to develop her feminine characteristics, which I often think are more valuable than anything we males have to offer, but was always devoting all her energies to getting the better of men. It was a characteristic that I did not find endearing at all."

"It is said in the market," Quarshie told Percy, "that she was in some kind of trouble with the local fetish."

"Who told you that?"

"A taxi driver."

"Yosofo," Mrs. Quarshie offered.

"Ah. A bright young man connected to the stool family, who were cheated out of their rightful aspirations to the local chieftancy. Which fetisher was he talking about?"

Quarshie wrinkled his brow and looked at his wife.

"Babalayou," she said.

"So? That old rogue. You perhaps know the expression 'When Greeks joined Greeks, then there was a tug of war,' Doctor?"

Quarshie shook his head.

"Nathaniel Lee, a Restoration dramatist . . . it comes from *Theodosius,* no, *The Rival Queens* . . . which is all beside the point . . . I am showing off. Anyway, the thought expresses the situation quite clearly. If they clashed I would not think that either of them was up to any good."

"How powerful is Babalayou here in the town?"

"I expect there are a lot of people who are afraid of him."

"To the extent that they might kill for him if he ordered it?"

"Doctor, I have spent almost all my adult life in Africa. Your people are very . . . 'suggestible' is I think the word . . . as, of course, are people everywhere. In Europe and America it is the advertising people and the politicians who make fools of them. Here, it's again the politicians and what are vulgarly called the juju men. I would never commit myself to a statement about the powers of this or that fetisher. Why don't you go and see him and judge him for yourself? Your instincts will be more reliable than mine."

"Yes, I intend to, though I suspect that in matters of instinct, your capabilities are vastly superior to mine, just as is your knowledge of such items as these."

Quarshie brought out the three pieces of gold and handed them to Percy, who took them casually, and then, when he saw what they were, his attitude changed. His casualness became clearly deliberate.

His first words were spoken very quietly. He said, "Interesting. There is a magnifying glass on the table behind you. I would be grateful if you would hand it to me." Then he scrutinised each piece, his eyes riveted on the objects under the lens.

Eventually he put the glass down and handed the gold back to Quarshie, and his scrutiny of the doctor was as intense as it had been of the gold.

Quarshie matched the old man's impassivity.

From where Mrs. Quarshie sat it looked as if they were playing a game, each wary, each waiting for the other to show some sign of his next move.

Quarshie won.

"Where did you get these?"

"For the moment I cannot tell you because I don't know what they are and therefore how important they might be to my investigation."

Percy nodded. "I accept that," he said. "Ultimately I would suggest that they will be more valuable to me than to you. To the human race as a whole they might even be more valuable than the life of a female American journalist. But at the moment I respect your caution. And when I said valuable, I did not mean in the pecuniary sense. Gold is gold, although old gold has an even greater financial value. My interest is historical. I don't need money. I am eighty-one years old. This is my home. Out there on the hill which overlooks the river and the country beyond it, my grave is already dug. My concern is only to add to man's knowledge of the world, particularly the past."

Quarshie weighed the gold in his hand and asked, "What are they?"

"Precisely, I don't know. But if you go quite a long way northeast from here along one of the trails which still lead across the Sahara you will come to a place called Oualata. There, though you are surrounded by rocky cliffs, you will find sweet water and a settlement. Once it was quite an important stop on the caravan route to the north and then to the east. It was the route Mansa Musa took on his way to Cairo. At Oualata, amongst the ruins, you will find designs on the walls exactly like those that have been cast, there, in gold. Musa, or perhaps some other traveller of the same period, brought the designs back with him from ancient Egypt. I suspect they are unique. It is the first time I have seen those patterns reproduced in that way. That's as far as my knowledge goes."

"Are there other people in the neighbourhood who might have your kind of interest in them?"

"I doubt it, but you never know. If they are what I think they are there will be collectors who will be prepared to pay wildly inflated prices for such things, prices which will be greater than a hundred times the value of their natural weight in gold. Does anyone else know you have them?"

"I don't think so."

"And where are you going to keep them?"

"That is a decision I intend to make tomorrow morning."

"Then have a care. The price of that kind of gold is too often measured in blood. But perhaps you know that and it is the reason you have showed your find to me?"

CHAPTER SEVEN

"He has a house amongst the rocks far from the town.
Few have ever seen it and lived to speak of it."

The huts, nine of them, stood in a circle. They had thatched roofs and were connected by a thick hedge of camel thorn which was more impenetrable than heavy barbed wire. The compound harked back to an age before men used guns, when marauding lions and hyenas frequently raided human settlements for supplies of fresh meat.

Every family in the village, which was scattered over an area of more than a square mile, possessed a similar fortified collection of round huts, though the household that Quarshie had just entered was larger than most because it belonged to a family which frequently provided the tribe with its chiefs. The entrance to the compound was through the one rectangular building in the complex and housed a massive doorway that was a miniature of those which once served as entrances to small fortified towns in medieval Europe.

Quarshie, for this visit, had changed out of his Western clothes and was wearing a purple cloth edged with gold embroidery. It was draped across his torso like a roman toga, leaving one handsomely muscled shoulder bare. As he entered the compound he had to stoop slightly because the gate had not been built for men who were over six feet tall.

Yosofo had also changed his clothes and instead of the ubiquitous white shirt and khaki pants was now wearing the traditional white cloth, which hung from his shoulders almost to his heels and was wide enough to reach his wrists, if he stretched his arms out horizontally on each side of him, though it was split down each side from top to bottom. On his head he wore a soft white hat shaped like a cloche.

Quarshie was on his way to visit Yosofo's grandmother's sister Anoma, the woman Yosofo had said "heard the most."

He was by himself because Levitsky had called on Mrs. Quarshie to help him. The doctor had been summoned to attend more deliveries than he could handle, his usual midwife being amongst them.

Quarshie knew that Anoma would be one of the most important people in the tribe. It was a situation in which traditional custom triumphed over that of an imported religion. Obedience to ancient tribal customs was the rule rather than the exception with those in West Africa who appeared to have been converted to Christianity or, in this case, Islam. These converts celebrated the rites and ceremonials of the new religions enthusiastically but in their hearts they carefully preserved their own beliefs concerning the magical powers of all gods, their own and those of the foreigners who conquered them.

The entrance of the hut towards which Yosofo led Quarshie was protected from the rest of the compound by a three-foot-high wall attached to the side of the hut in the shape of an arc. It had been built to keep the goats and speckled guinea fowl from intruding into the living space and was a common feature of most of the huts. One part of the red mud wall in front of the entrance into the hut had been polished until it shone by the passage of people's buttocks as, with their backs to the wall, they jumped up to take a seat on it and then swivelled around to drop down on the other side. A small free-standing ladder was available for those too old or too young to make the passage over the wall in the accepted way.

The door into the hut itself was no more than a large hole, which made it necessary for those visiting to go on all fours before they could enter. Once inside Quarshie found that the only light came from this hole and from another in the centre of the roof which served as a vent and a chimney.

Women of the age, rank and dignity of the old lady who inhabited the hut were regarded, whether they actually held the position or not, as the queen mother and were therefore exonerated from the need to tend fires in the communal kitchen and allowed to have a fire of their own.

After coming out of the sun it took some moments for Quarshie's eyes to adjust to the darkness within the hut. And even when he began to be able to see the light was so dim that he could not be sure what he was looking at. As far as he could tell the whole circumference wall was hung from the ceiling to the clean-swept mud floor with nets containing brightly polished, golden globes that were often as much as two feet in diameter. In the darkness, however, it was impossible to tell what the globes were made of.

Noticing Quarshie's puzzled expression as he looked around, Yosofo told him, "Gourds. My grandmother's personal fortune. They are some of the biggest and best that can be found from here to Bambako."

The only other furnishing visible was a sleeping mat made of hollow reeds tied together in bundles to form a mattress several inches thick.

When his eyes were finally adjusted Quarshie discovered the old woman he had come to see sitting on a low stool.

Except for a short white cloth hanging between her legs she was naked and skeletally thin. She appeared to Quarshie to be over eighty years old and she sat motionlessly with her eyes, which had milky brown irises, fixed unblinkingly on him.

Through her grandson Quarshie gave her a conventional greeting and continued as she, still unblinking, murmured the traditional responses. Quarshie waited respectfully for her to begin the conversation.

She was not, however, in any hurry but continued to stare at him until he felt that, though she never looked away from his face, she had measured and taken in his every physical dimension and had probed into his mind to discover all that there was to know of him and his present intentions.

At last, continuing to speak her own language, and waiting for her grandson to translate each sentence, she said, "Your curiosity is strong in you, big man. Do you believe I can satisfy it?"

"If you wish to, mother, I believe you can."

"What do you want me to tell you?"

"As much as you can of the behaviour of certain men and women."

"Like the white one who died out there on the rocks? You

are from the coast sent by the big man there to find out about that woman's well-deserved end. Is that not so?"

"How do you sift the falsehoods out of the truths of what you are told, mother?"

"It is a matter of having an eye, a mind and the memory which enables you to look at a pot and tell how much water it will hold. The truth must fit the shape of what exists. Is that not true of the work you do, big man?"

"It is."

"And the others you will want to know about are Babalayou, the white one with the pictures of naked women on his arms and the other who often crosses the boundary of our land where it meets the boundary of our neighbour's land, at night." Yosofo turned to Quarshie and added, "I think my grandmother is speaking of the Frenchman."

"Tell her, yes, I want to hear about all those and any others besides them who may try to hide their actions from the sight of honest men."

For a moment there was a glimmer of a smile on Anoma's face as she asked, "Are you prepared, then, to stay with me until the moon rises and sets again? For the honest are few in number and those who are deceivers are many."

"Mother, it is said by my people that the man who fails to examine every stitch in a garment may fail to notice the very one that is broken and may cause it to fall apart."

"So? But you will not be able to make a whole garment out of the fragments about each person that I shall be able to give you."

"A fragment, mother, will tell me the colour and the pattern of the cloth and from that I shall know whether what I find belongs to this one or that one."

"Good. Then, a fragment on the white woman. She was several times seen accompanying the white man who crosses the desert at night by paths known only to a few of our people."

"On foot?"

"It was said that they went in a car."

"Who knows these paths besides the white man?"

There was a moment's silence before Yosofo said, "I, for one, know them, sir, but my grandmother does not know that I do."

"They are used by smugglers?"

"As you say, sir."

"What do you smuggle?"

"A few small things."

"You talk freely of it?"

"It is no secret, sir. Every man here who has a car brings things into and out of Transniger across these tracks."

"What things?"

"There the government does not subsidise the price of ground nuts; here it does. I can make enough money on a sack of ground nuts to pay the cost of fuel for two months."

"And the other way?"

"The Transniger Government is very strict about the import of liquor. The leaders follow Islam more strictly there than they do here. So a bottle of beer, there, sells for twice the price it does here. Neither activities do harm to any persons, sir. Rather they signify the stupidity of the men who make the laws."

"You should have gone to university as you said you wanted to and afterwards you could have gone on to join the government and make wise laws."

"Such laws, sir, should not be made by central governments. The people, wherever they live, should make their own laws. In this way much that is foolish would be done away with."

Anoma said something rather sharply and Yosofo looked abashed.

"What did she say?"

"She told me that she could see that the lion cub was trying to teach its father how to hunt. I meant no disrespect, sir."

"Of course. You must speak your mind to me whenever you will. Now ask your grandmother whether she knows any more about the white woman, please."

Yosofo did as he was bid and after Anoma had replied he turned back to Quarshie and told him, "From all that she heard the only other thing that Mama Anoma wants to say is that she was a woman who pleased herself in all that she did and that, to her, others were simply dry wood that she used on her fire to warm herself and cook her food."

"And Babalayou?" Quarshie asked.

"Is a man who is like a stick driven into the sand." Yosofo continued to translate his grandmother's answers. "It depends on the position of the sun for the direction in which it throws its shadow. He is subtle in his understanding of men and coarse in the way he deals with them. Often, very often, he cheats them. I can say such things of him because at my age death has become a close neighbour, a familiar, and I have no fear of him because I am quite ready to join the ancestors."

"What about the Anglis one who builds bridges?"

"There is a man who is and always has been an enemy to our people. It is said that he practices magic and makes people disappear. People fear for their children when he is near. It is also said that he has a house, amongst the rocks far from the town. Few have ever seen it and lived to speak of it. Of such as he there are many stories. One is that he can use two women at once. Though no woman I have heard of has been used this way."

"And the old man, the white, who lives with his machine for making a great noise?"

"*He* is a man. Many years ago, when I and he were younger, we lay together." Again the fleeting suggestion of a smile passed over Anoma's face. "My husband needed information that could only be obtained from a man in govmint. He, who is now like me, old, needed information that he could get only from the chief, my husband. So, you could say, I lay between them facing both ways at once and thus knew twice as much as they did. Men are not clever."

"What about the white doctor and his wife?"

"He is the only man I have ever allowed to put his hands inside me knowing that his only purpose was to do good for me. Him I trust."

"The district officer?"

"Is vain and a fool. Anyone who is clever and patient can

use him. But you asked of the doctor's woman and did not wait for my answer. She is halfway to her ancestors already. Only her feet walk on the ground; her head is with those who were here before us so she has no eyes for seeing our world, yours and mine."

Quarshie said, "So much you see and know yet you never step out of the darkness of this house."

Anoma shrugged slightly. "Here, in my house, without the need to watch where I set my feet, or to count my words when I speak, or to have a care to listen to so much that shakes the air but has no meaning, here I can turn every piece of information I receive so that it catches the light in a hundred different ways. I have time, even, to turn it inside out if I want to. For these reasons, big man, I have the time to look for truth and that requires that I have time to examine all that is not true. Also I have learned that truth is a two-fold experience. It is a fact and it is what we think about the fact."

"When people talk of sages, mother, they always seem to be talking of men and they are foolish. You have proved to me how foolish they are. Now, one last question. I have heard stories that are still being told of there being much gold under the sands somewhere to the north of this town. Do you know anything of that matter?"

"Only that it must be true because I have seen pieces of gold that had not been worked by our people. It is like the years when there are no rains. No one can say when they will occur or why. One day a man comes to the town with a few gold pieces. Then for years there is none. Why? Why does it happen like that? No one can say. Like the rain . . . one year it comes . . . another year it stays away."

"And you do not know where the gold comes from?"

"Not exactly, only that it seems to be within territory such as a man might cover walking ten days from north to south and fourteen, or fifteen, east to west. It is a great area."

Quarshie felt as if he had been given many columns of figures to add up and none of them seemed to come out with a sensible answer.

It was very strange. He would simply have to go on collecting figures and doing his sums.

He thanked Anoma for her patience and help and told her he would come back and see her again.

"Those who come to see me speak well of your woman," Anoma said as he left. "When you come again bring her with you." It was an order and Quarshie promised that he would obey it.

CHAPTER EIGHT

"If a lion planned to hunt for his dinner by a certain water hole would he send to all the deer in the neighbourhood to tell them of the place and time he proposed to take his meat?"

When Quarshie went to see him the police superintendent received the doctor with the minimum of courtesy needed to avoid confrontation.

After a very formal greeting the superintendent explained his view of Quarshie's mission. He asked how Quarshie would feel if a policeman was sent to run his clinic and he was ordered to play a subordinate role. And he left the question that was the natural corollary to that one, concerning his own situation in Norenga, unasked.

Quarshie made sympathetic sounds without committing himself to a direct answer for fear of starting an argument.

The superintendent then explained that he still had plenty of other work to do, thanked the doctor for coming to see him and invited him to get on with the job of finding the man who had killed the white woman and leave him to carry out those aspects of his work which had not been taken away from him.

As a parting shot he added, darkly, that it was bad enough to have, as a district officer, a man who did not take matters of law and order seriously and who set the community a bad example without having his authority as superintendent undermined by having amateurs sent into his district to do his work for him. At that point, obviously under great emotional stress, he stood up, said, "Good day, Dr. Quarshie," and left the room.

Quarshie did a lot better with Babalayou.

The old witch doctor's most obvious characteristics were the thoughtful way in which he spoke and his curiosity. In another society and given the right means, he might have become a scientist and a scholar.

His face was covered with skin that was the colour of dark ox blood and as shiny as well-polished leather. His jaw bones were as boldly cast as those of a horse, his eyes were slits which displayed no whites and his mouth and lips were also equine in their fullness and mobility. In short, he was a very ugly old man and probably, Quarshie thought, a very corrupt one.

However, since a large part of Babalayou's time was spent in treating corruption in those who came to see him, catering to their acquisitiveness and their jealousies as well as their fears of these same characteristics in other people, it was not surprising that he had been infected by this experience.

To a man from the south Babalayou's surroundings were as unfamiliar as the alleys and courtyards of an Arab souk might have been to a man born and raised in one of the villages of northern Europe. His compound was tightly enclosed by massive walls which, since they were built of mud and had to withstand deluging floods of water during the short rainy season, were buttressed on the outside with structures resembling the bastions that stood around the walls of fortified medieval towns in Europe. The only entrance to the compound was through a single narrow door.

Inside, the stamped earth where it was open to the sky was kept as immaculate as the floors within the surrounding rooms. In the centre of the courtyard, there was a shrine, a small, white-painted dome of mud encircled by various sacred objects, a gaily painted hoe, several pots of different sizes, two figures woven out of straw, a variety of animal bones and skulls, small leather pouches containing herbs, coloured stones, samples of earth and ashes and compounds of various kinds of organic matter. All these articles had different symbolic meanings in the same way that plaster figures, wine, bread, silver medals, mitres, rings, black skull caps and ikons have symbolic values in other religions.

Beside the shrine there were also two low stools and a wooden board marked with more or less geometrical patterns. With elaborate courtesy the old man invited Quarshie to sit on one of the stools.

Being watched by the witch doctor was, Quarshie decided, like being watched through a slit in the concrete wall of a fortress by a man behind a machine gun. Make the wrong move and you would have to jump for your life.

Martha, he thought, must have been very insensitive or else very brave to risk arousing the antagonism of a man of Babalayou's subtlety and skill.

Having completed the correct rituals involved in receiving and giving greetings, Quarshie decided to throw the old man off his stride by taking a direct and therefore unconventional approach.

"Did you make good your threat to kill the white woman who took away your *Kadou* brasses, father?" he asked.

Babalayou's gaze did not waver. In a soft voice he replied, "There are ways to catch chickens, my son, and there are ways to catch hares. The man who uses the method suitable for catching a chicken to catch a hare will catch nothing but the wind the hare leaves by its passage." He was rebuking Quarshie for thinking he could surprise him into making a rash statement.

Quarshie persisted, "We are not talking of hares or chickens, father, but a white woman and her death has created so much palaver that the big man, who is the biggest of them all and lives in Port St. Mary, has sent me to you to ask if you did this thing you boasted you were going to do."

"If a lion planned to hunt for his dinner by a certain water hole would he send to all the deer in the neighbourhood to tell them of the place and the time where he proposed to take his meat? My son, first you treat me like a chicken and then you ask if I am a fool. Do you expect to find answers to your problems in that way?"

"Father, a man cannot know the depth of a pool unless he has taken a stick and driven it down through the water until it strikes the bottom."

They were both speaking in Hausa and Babalayou nodded his head and said, "Now I hear you, my son. Now I hear you. You are speaking in a tongue which I understand, a tongue which tells me that you are of the same people that I am and not one of those from across the water."

"But it is those who are across the water who can cause the greatest trouble over the death of that woman."

"Then let them teach their people manners and behaviour that is respectful and not full of pride because they have more money and therefore think they own the world and everyone in it. See, I spit on that female's memory." And he did so, launching a gob of saliva that dried quickly in the sun into a dark stain on the terra-cotta soil.

"Spittle will not wash away the memory of her death, father, until it is known who killed her and why. Is there anything you can tell me that will help me find the one who took her life?"

"I can tell you the part I played in the affair and afterwards we can ask the ancestors what they can tell us of it."

"I came prepared with offerings for the ancestors, father." Quarshie took a bottle of gin out of a bag and a handful of kola nuts which he laid on the ground on a ten-beni note.

Babalayou took the gin, opened it and poured a little on the ground for the ancestors. Then he drank directly from the bottle and passed it to Quarshie for him to do the same. He ignored the kola nuts and the money.

"For my part, my son," he said, after a few moments of thoughtful silence, "I put a curse on her and on the man who brought her to me."

"The district officer?"

"The same."

"Why him?"

"Because he had become a part of her. When you cut down a palm in which weaver birds nest you must cut down the whole tree for if you leave any part of it you might as well not cut it down at all because the birds will come back to it and then go to other palms and blight them. So, putting the curse on her was my part. Now"—he took the board with the geometric patterns on it and a handful of cowrie shells—"we will ask the ancestors what they can tell us." He threw the shells with a gesture similar to that of a man who throws dice and then studied the way the cowries fell. For a long time he sat quite still and once or twice he closed his eyes as if to clear his visual screen of all the other images which were printed on it.

After a few moments he said, "I am directed to contact your noma."

Amongst the tribe who inhabited the region around Norenga and were nominally Muslims Quarshie knew that the noma was said to be that part of a man's entity which "rides across the lake of time on his soul." It is the element of a man's nature which he constructs out of his experiences, his thoughts and memories. An infant does not have a noma. It forms slowly at different ages in different individuals, thus accounting for the fact that some people are more able than others.

A noma may also live on after a man's death but its survival depends on his achievements during his lifetime and whether or not he is warmly remembered by those who knew him. In the instance of a man who is not so remembered his noma perishes soon after him.

It is believed that a man's noma rides a few days ahead of his soul in his journey through life so it can warn him, through his premonitions, through his dreams, or through a soothsayer, of the dangers which lie in wait for him. It was considered that the soothsayer was often the best means of making this contact because it required certain trained sensibilities which were lacking in most people.

Babalayou closed his eyes and after a while, when he started to speak, there was a suggestion that he had been transformed into a puppet and that the voice which came out of his mouth was using him as a megaphone to deliver a message which originated in another dimension.

The voice said, "I and I, who are one in we, declare that what lies ahead in our destiny is such that it would cause lesser men to turn back. The force we confront is death both for ourselves and for others. Some will certainly die and the force which turns life into death and returns it to the source of all things waits in the cool shade of the rocks and in the heat of the peak of noon. So, to live, we, I and I who are one, must remember that skin, whether it is white or black and though it is only a thin covering, conceals a man's heart, the one that is evil as well as the one that is friendly."

There was a pause, then Babalayou said in his normal voice, "It is all, my son. What did your noma tell you?"

"You do not hear what it says, father?"

"It is not my voice you listen to when I am used thus, rather it is as if I am dead. A man could strike me with an axe and I would not know it. So what did your noma tell you?"

Quarshie repeated the message.

"Then you would be wise to take a medicine which will give you protection against those who have evil in their hearts. I will make and give you some."

Quarshie thought how similar the role the old man played was to the one played by a medical practitioner in the Western world. The patient was not consulted about the specifics he was given but told, "Here, take this, it will make you better. It is what you need."

What Babalayou gave him was a small flat canvas bag that was sealed. Quarshie was to wear it around his neck on a leather thong. He was not given any information about what it contained or how it would work.

"It" cost twenty-five benis and he was expected to be grateful for it.

When Quarshie got back to the rest house his wife was already there. She was on edge with impatience to tell him something and when she asked him what he had been doing her question was perfunctory. So he answered her briefly and then asked how her day had gone.

It was as if he had pulled a cork out of a champagne bottle.

Dr. Levitsky had left her in charge of the maternity clinic. She had heard a lot of interesting things. She had discovered how society, as it applied to the women in and around Norenga, worked.

"It is just like Port St. Mary," she said, "even though it is much smaller. 'Walk-about women' are just as plentiful."

The term "walk-about women" came to Akhana from another West African country and had a broader meaning than prostitution. It could be used to describe any woman who is promiscuous but it did not carry any undertones of opprobrium. It was used to describe women who refused to be governed by man-made laws. The need for sex was regarded as an appetite akin to hunger and thirst. The only difference being that, in its truest form, its satisfaction required the co-operation of someone of the opposite sex. There were, however, some taboos connected with its satisfaction. Generally, they related to the need for a father to know that the children born to his wife were his children and therefore the need for wives to steer clear of adultery. Also there were stringent taboos, in most tribes, against bearing children out of wedlock.

"One thing here that is different," Mrs. Quarshie said, "is that Norenga being basically an Islamic neighbourhood there is a special quarter, a *zongo,* for foreign prostitutes, most of whom are here on their own without family or friends."

"So?" Quarshie asked.

"So, if they disappear nobody bothers very much. It is assumed that they have gone home or moved to some other place where they think they can make more money."

Mrs. Quarshie paused to see if her husband was acute enough to pick up the direction in which she was heading. He was.

"And some of those you talked to are suspicious that those who disappear do so for other reasons?" he asked.

"Yes."

"Were you able to find anyone who had any positive evidence?"

"How could I, Quarshie, I was stuck in the clinic all the time. But I did find out who might be able to give us more information. You see, there have been rows between the women in the *zongo* area and local walk-about women, so both sides elected one of their own constituency to represent them in disputes. The one in the *zongo* is called a *magajiya* and it is her duty not only to represent the women in the *zongo* when they get into trouble with the locals but also to receive complaints from women who have been cheated out of their fees, to fix those fees in agreement with the local girls and so on. The *magajiya* is recognised by the local chief, who officially installs her and gives her a special turban to mark her status. She can actually fine customers who default on payment as well as recover the fees they failed to pay. She is the woman we should see."

It was very hot and Quarshie was tired.

Mrs. Quarshie was too full of her own excitement to notice it. She said, "Shall we go, now?"

Quarshie was not quite sure whether the trail Mrs. Quarshie had discovered related to his investigation, but he did not want to dampen her enthusiasm and he was chary of ignoring her instincts, which had frequently proved sound.

"We will eat, relax a little, then we will go," he told her.

The *magajiya,* when the Quarshies called on her, turned out to be an imposing woman of great dignity and probably, Quarshie thought, of great shrewdness.

They had to wait until the evening to make their call because during the day she was responsible for a stall in the market place though she did not attend it herself but supplied *tuwo* and various spiced sauces called *miya* as well as *marmare,* which the Hausa regard as snacks. She employed a young Fulani girl to sell these items.

She was probably a little beyond middle age and Quarshie felt that he should offer to pay her for her time. It was an offer she refused. She told him that the market was buzzing with the story that he was in Norenga and the fact that he had visited her would make her an important woman. It was a statement that was made with a smile. Both the Quarshies felt at ease with her immediately though the tribal markings on her face indicated that she was a Hausa woman and, as such, as foreign in her traditions and life-style to her visitors as a native of the cattle lands in Texas would be to a native of the Bronx. Perhaps this was because she and the Quarshies seemed to share a natural liberality in their approach towards people whether the latter judged themselves to be their superiors or their inferiors. "She is," Quarshie said afterwards, "in the best sense, a woman of humility but one whom it would be impossible to humiliate." Mrs. Quarshie, when she had digested his statement, agreed with him.

The house she occupied was small but had a well-watered garden and was furnished with rather heavy, old-fashioned furniture in a more or less European style.

As well as a girl to market her produce she also employed a young girl to tend the fires in the yard at the back of the house where the cooking was done.

Her name, she told Quarshie, was Ladidi.

"You work hard," he said.

"Night and day, *dono*," she replied, again with a smile and using a form of address for Quarshie that is normally used only for those who are to be feared such as chiefs, other powerful persons and even evil spirits. "A hare is not to be caught by sitting down."

As he translated for his wife Quarshie told her that hard work is greatly admired amongst the Hausa and he repeated another well-known proverb which said the same thing, "*Su babu tsaraka wanka ne*. Fishing without a net is bathing," he translated for her.

"You speak our tongue well, *dono*," Ladidi said.

"One needs to if one is not to be misunderstood, *iya*," Quarshie replied, using a highly complimentary form of address for the senior woman in a neighbourhood.

"Your man go speak plenty fine Hausa, mama," Ladidi told Mrs. Quarshie in pidgin.

Quarshie laughed and said to Mrs. Quarshie, "We are flattering each other. But to speak good Hausa is very tricky. For instance, the word *kashi* pronounced one way can mean a 'thrashing.' Pronounced another way it can mean 'soaked to the skin.' Pronounced a third way it can mean 'gambling.' And most dangerous of all, said in a fourth way it can mean 'excrement.'" Then turning back to Ladidi, he said, "But we did not come here to make word gifts to each other, *iya,* but to ask information of you."

"About the *nasara* who was beaten to death in the wilderness?"

"*Nasrani* is the Arabic word for Christian," Quarshie told his wife, "the Hausa have made it into *nasara.*" To Ladidi he said, "That thing, *iya,* and also about the women of this neighbourhood. We hear that some of them are disappearing and no one knows where they have gone."

The placid expression that had occupied Ladidi's seemingly imperturbable features changed only very slightly. "So that is your first interest, *dono?*" she asked. "Is it permitted that I should know why?"

"It is my experience, *iya,* that when several mysterious events occur in one place and at one time they are often connected."

"You must get your information from the spirits for I have spoken of this connection between the white woman and those who are disappearing to no one. But, as you say, they must be connected because the white woman came to me asking many questions and amongst them the one you are asking now. She also made me swear not to speak of her questions and she paid me well. Now that she is dead I am freed of that oath."

"What exactly did she want to know?"

"The same, I tell you, that you asked."

"And what did you reply?"

"*Dono,* I know very little. In the past three years some twenty-five women who worked here have left. Eight of these I have heard of again that they are in this place, or that. Of the others I have heard nothing."

"Were those of whom you heard nothing of the same tribe?"

"No, *dono,* but they were of about the same age. That is young, and some of them took the girls who worked for them with them, children you understand, not yet in bud."

"And you just accepted their disappearance without reporting it to the police or the district officer?"

"*Dono,* to speak with such important men—yes, even to

speak with them—I must take an offering to them and that offering has to be my own body."

"And the chief?"

For a little while Ladidi looked at her hands, which lay in her lap. When she looked up it was to stare hard into Quarshie's eyes and he felt that her pause had covered the time it took her to decide whether or not she could trust him. She said, "He is young, *dono,* he spends much money but does not have much and . . ." She paused again uncertainly.

"And," Quarshie prompted. "*Iya,* you can trust me. I am not of this place. I have no allegiances here to any man and want only to do what is right."

"I feel it, *dono,* and I have had much experience of men. This young man came to his chieftaincy only last year and there are many who believe that though he has washed them publicly there is blood on his hands and . . . many of those girls who have disappeared were summoned to see him and came back richer, much richer, though it is known that the chief himself has little wealth."

"So where might he get his money from?"

"*Dono,* if you find the answer to that question you may well find the answer to many others."

When they were alone again together at the rest house Mrs. Quarshie said, "I was right, wasn't I? There could be a connection, couldn't there, between the disappearance of those girls and Martha's death?"

Quarshie smiled and said nothing.

"Couldn't there?" Mrs. Quarshie insisted. "You weren't too keen about going to see her at first, were you? Were you?"

Quarshie put his arm around her and said, "Of course you're right and the answer to every question is yes." Then he added slyly, "And that Madam Ladidi is a very attractive woman."

Mrs. Quarshie stuck out her tongue at him and found herself on her back on the bed so swiftly that the only thing she could say was, "Why do expats call this horseplay? I am sure horses don't know anything about it at all."

CHAPTER NINE

A small flat piece of rock painted with gilt and a very blood-soaked piece of paper . . .

Quarshie was up before dawn and, as the first light spread across the sky ahead of the sun, he experienced the unique moment of silence which comes to many parts of the tropics at that hour. The night belongs to the invertebrates, the insects, and they fill every nook and cranny of it with millions of tiny vibrations. The sounds they make are almost subliminal and the human mind becomes aware that they have been there only after they have stopped.

Then, just before sunrise, there is a pause after the insects switch off and animals, including man, come gradually back to life and create sounds which are far less co-ordinated and therefore more penetrating. The contrast, to one conscious of it, is as marked as the contrast which exists between the northern and southern faces of Norenga.

To the south is the river. The water which flows between its banks is red and along its margins small plantations of mangoes and orange groves fill out a variety of geometric forms in several hundred acres.

To the north the country is fiercely barren. From the slight eminence, on which the rest house is set, the main features are the rocks and the colour of the soil. The latter, like the river, is red and everything grows out of it and is made of it, huts, roads, mosques, walls, communal ovens, dyeing pits and the minute scraps of cultivated land set between rocks.

Yosofo, who was to pick up Karago, the old hunter, and then drive Quarshie out to the site where Martha had been murdered, was late.

When he arrived the sun was already above the horizon, piercing the slight haze with a force which suggested that it had awoken in a rage and was determined to make every living creature suffer for it.

Yosofo said he had a lot of trouble finding Karago, who had

been visiting relatives on the other side of the river. Now the
old man sat uncomfortably in the back of the taxi nursing a
carbine, a short rifle which, Quarshie had once been told, had
been used in cavalry regiments around the turn of the century.
The rest of Karago's accoutrements consisted of his genet-skin
apron and the leather pouch he carried on a thong slung over
his shoulder. His chest and shoulders were bare and he wore no
shoes or sandals. The pouch, Quarshie discovered later, contained homemade ammunition and a little sun-dried meat that
could only have been slightly less tough than his genet skin had
Karago ever tried to eat it.

The air, as they drove northwards through the outskirts of
the town, smelt of burning cow dung and the heat already
seemed to make the dusty air vibrate. After a mud mosque with
its towers decorated symmetrically with protruding balks of
timber as if it were armoured to impale attackers . . . some of
the balks, during the heaviest rains, spouted water with the
force of a fire hose; after passing an old gentleman on his knees
by the side of the road, facing Mecca, saying his prayers next to
a man noisily beating copper into ornaments; after meeting the
professional beggars, mostly blind, being led out by small boys
to do their day's work of chanting passages from the Koran
with their hands held out for donations; after noting that feminine seductiveness in Norenga was promoted by the display of
one beautiful shoulder with a matt gleam on skin the colour of
a purple plum . . . an enticing display that was achieved by
wearing a bodice with a wide neck line which was allowed to
slip sideways; after passing a number of houses carefully decorated in several colours with patterns somewhat like the ones
which decorated the pieces of gold Mrs. Quarshie had found in
Martha's hairbrush; after nearly running down several goats
and many chickens; after these early morning sights and sounds
the land became barren and void of anything except rocks, sand
and the blinding glare of the sunlight.

Unusual for him, Quarshie was wearing a soft cloth hat. It
was green and the narrow brim was turned down all around so
that it fitted over his head in the shape of a bell and came low

over his forehead and the back of his neck. He had expected
Yosofo to be late so he was prepared to walk to the site during
the hours when the sun fell on men's heads and shoulders like
liquid fire.

"Karago speaks Hausa, not so?" Quarshie asked Yosofo.

"Yes, sir. He is not a Hausaman but comes from the Mussi
people. However, he was born here so Hausa comes more easily to him than Mussi."

Quarshie turned in the front seat and spoke to the hunter.
"Old one, I have no doubt you have seen much in your years?"
His intonation made a question of his words.

"I have, *dono*. Most of what the sun has seen and much of
what the moon has seen has passed before my eyes."

"Watchful eyes?"

"Indeed, *dono,* when a man hunts for a living he must use
his eyes like a dog uses the wind. For him no scent is too feeble
to be noticed; for me no grain of sand is too small to escape attention."

"Did you tell the white doctor and the police all that you
saw when you found the dead woman?"

"They thought their own eyes were good enough, *dono,* so
they did not ask."

Yosofo swerved to avoid a deep pothole, skidded on the
road's sandy surface and recovered control of the car with
highly practiced skill. The lurch threw the hunter off his balance and Quarshie saw that he put all his effort into saving his
gun from knocking against anything but took, without wincing,
quite a blow on his shoulder.

"What did you see, old one, that the others did not see?"

"I have not their eyes, *dono,* so I cannot answer that question. But I can tell you what they did not look at."

"What was that?"

"The trail back to where the woman fell and the place where
she fell."

"But you did?"

"It was the way I came to the body. I told them of it but the
doctor did not seem to think it was important. He said he was

very hot and very tired. Nor did the govmint man want me to guide him over the way I had been."

"Will you be able to find the trail again now?"

"Even when it is two or three months old I shall be able to find it. The sand out here is not like the land around a compound in the town where children and old women sweep it clean every morning."

Yosofo said, "You will discover, yourself, sir, how hot it gets out here. If we can, we should be on our way home before the heat reaches its worst."

Quarshie doubted that they would, but he said nothing. Thinking about the old man's comment, it occurred to him that neither Levitsky nor Ephraim would have been seriously concerned about finding the murderer when they saw Martha's body for the first time. They would have been, as Levitsky had pointed out, in a considerable state of shock and just possibly the doctor might even have experienced a sense of relief and thought it best to leave things alone, while Ephraim, already overloaded with work, would have preferred to leave the investigation to someone else. And that was what had happened. Levitsky had done the P.M. and written his report and Ephraim had contacted Jedawi as quickly as he possibly could. There, they could both have said, their responsibilities ended.

Owing to the condition of the road, it took them almost two hours to cover the forty miles to the place where Karago indicated they should turn off towards the west. Quarshie was not able to see what had sign-posted the spot for the hunter. The dirt highway, lined on each side with a jumbled array of splintered rocks, rubble and sand, stretched as far as the eye could see. It was as featureless as a cart track through a ploughed field.

As they got out of the car to start walking Quarshie asked the hunter to be allowed to look at his gun. The old man would not let him have it but turned it lovingly in his hands so that Quarshie could examine it closely. It was obviously given the care that a master violinist would bestow on a perfect Stradivarius. As a last proud gesture Karago operated the bolt and, with his thumbnail in the breach to reflect the light, invited Quarshie to look down the barrel. The inside of the gun gleamed as if every millimeter of it was polished though Quarshie saw what he, a man with little knowledge of guns, thought to be a defect. It seemed as if the rifling had worn unevenly.

He said, "I can see that it is the most important of your children, old man, and is cared for in a manner that is fitting to one who has such great importance."

"*Dono,* no child has repaid its parent's care better than this one. There have been occasions when it has saved my family from starvation. Only"—Karago sighed and looked disconsolate—"it is old, as I am, and it does not shoot quite as straight as it did."

It was the opening Quarshie wanted. He said, "Help me well, my friend, and I will see that you get a new gun which will shoot as straight as you can see. It is a promise."

"I will serve you the best way I can, *dono,* but am sorry that I am not younger for then I could serve you better."

As he followed Karago from the road towards the place where Martha had been buried Quarshie felt the sun drenching the world with a fiery heat that was reflected back by the rocks. Like cheese in a toasted sandwich, he felt that at any moment he would melt. More accurately, perhaps, the sun was a hammer, the rocks were an anvil and between them their purpose was to crush him as Martha had been crushed. Why? Because all humans who wandered into this, or other areas of the desert, were intruders with no right to be there.

Fantasy? Modify it, then, he told himself and say that no one had a right to be there until, like Karago, they served a long hard apprenticeship, one that could well span generations.

As if aware of Quarshie's thoughts the old man stopped and pointed at a little patch of sand. "Scorpions," he said, "they were fighting. We disturbed them. They knew of our approach. See?" He bent and traced without touching them, two tiny trails in the sand. "One stood here turning to face an enemy which circled him." He straightened up, adding, "Like men, they sometimes war on each other and kill."

Quarshie wondered why killing in a war differed from murder. One group of people felt threatened by another and attacked them, killing them. That was war. One man felt threatened by another, attacked him and killed him. That was murder.

Who was being threatened by Martha? Levitsky had admitted to feeling threatened. What about Ephraim?

"We are arrived, *dono*. There is the grave." The shallow depression was partly filled with drifted sand. Quarshie bent and brushed some of the loose surface aside. Beneath it, in places, there were discs and other shapes, flat, almost black, that were thin but baked hard, blood mixed with sand which had turned to the consistency of bricks.

"And the stones, *dono*. See?" Karago turned some of them so that Quarshie could look at the surface on which Martha's blood had dried.

"How was she dressed when you found her and how was she lying?"

"On her face. Her head was here with some white material, much covered with blood, on the back of her neck. Also the seat of her cotton trousers was tied over the back of her neck and knotted under her chin. *Dono,* it would seem that that was what the man used to drag her body here, the legs of her trousers."

"So the lower part of her body was without cover?"

"From this part of her back down"—Karago indicated the lumbar region of his spine—"she had no clothes. The white pad on the back of her neck was made of her knickers."

"Did they turn her over when they carried her to the road?"

"They did."

"What did you see then?"

"What a man would expect to see when he looks at a half-naked woman. It was clear also that she had been with her stomach to the ground when she was dragged over the rocks. Mostly that side of her body was without skin."

Both men spoke without emotion because the hunter and the doctor were accustomed to the sight of blood.

With Yosofo it was different. He took one look at the grave and moved out of earshot. A moment later he made an important discovery. In another little patch of sand Yosofo saw a T section of wood sticking a little way out of the ground. He did not touch it but called Quarshie.

The doctor looked down at it for a moment and had to restrain Karago from bending and pulling it out of the ground.

Carefully he cleared away the sand from around the rest of the shaft revealing a short-handled spade with a narrow rectangular blade. Holding it very gingerly by the centre of the shaft, he lifted it and looked closely at the steel. Along one edge, like the rocks that had lain on Martha's body, it bore stains which could have been blood.

He put it down carefully and said, "We will pick it up on the way back to the car. Don't touch it. I may be able to tell from the handle what man used it."

"Is that then some magic?" Karago asked.

"Fingerprints." It was Yosofo who answered. "It was used to bury her, not so, sir?"

"And perhaps to kill her. Dr. Levitsky said the back of her skull was broken. We will go on to the place where you say she was killed."

"Why did the man not bury the thing better, sir?"

"He was probably very upset, perhaps frightened by what he had done. Perhaps, too, he was in a hurry. The top of the handle was no doubt out of sight when he left it but the wind blew the sand away and revealed it."

As they walked on Quarshie thought that even if there were no decipherable fingerprints, and he would have to wait a long time for that to be established because the spade would have to be taken to Port St. Mary for tests, the discovery would give him a useful weapon, one with which he might goad the murderer into making a revealing move.

"See," Karago kept saying. "The man, or perhaps men, for

they could take one leg of the trousers each, passed this way. There is blood there, and there, and there."

Finally, after walking over an almost continuous surface of rock for about a mile he stopped on a slight eminence of sandstone that was of a different nature to its surroundings and said, "In this place she was killed. There are no tracks beyond it."

The place where they stood showed its age, like the face of a very ancient human shows the passage of the years, by being full of cracks and fissures.

"Here she lay for quite a long time, *dono*. There is much blood here at the bottom of this hole. Perhaps she bent down or lay over it to look down into it and, as you say, she was struck by the spade and fell with her head in this place so that the blood ran down into the hole."

The cleavage in the rock was about a foot wide and the sides sloped together to more or less close the rift three feet down.

Something caught Quarshie's eye at the bottom of the crack and he bent suddenly to get a better look.

At the same moment a nickel-coated fragment of lead ripped the air apart just where he had been standing. At almost the same moment Karago threw himself sideways at Quarshie's legs so that the big man fell.

"A gun," the old man told him. "Keep flat. A hunter is over there behind a rock."

A gun? Quarshie's attention changed focus slowly. He had been looking at something which glinted like gold at the bottom of the crevice in the rock. The sound which had torn the air a moment before must have been a bullet.

His mind took hold and he turned on his face and crawled a few yards in the direction the hunter had indicated. As he did so he heard the crack of a gun, and out of the corner of his eye he saw Yosofo, with a blank expression on his face, collapse to his knees and then fall sideways.

The hunter said, "Stay here, *dono*. In this place you are safe. The one with the gun cannot see you. Here, put your hat on this rock and in a moment, when I move, raise it a little above the ridge in front of you."

Quarshie said, "Yosofo. He . . ."

"He is dead or has lost his mind to darkness. I will surprise that man there. Remember, in a moment, raise your hat above this rock."

The old man had been busy all the time he had been speaking and Quarshie saw that with a leather thong he had tied his carbine on his back so that the stock rested below his shoulder blades and the barrel lay in the cleft of his buttocks.

Then, flatter on his belly than a snake, for he did not even raise his head but turned it so that one ear was on the ground, he said, "Now the hat, *dono*," and started to crawl away to the right.

Gingerly Quarshie pushed the rock with the hat on it above the ridge. After two or three seconds a shower of rock chips just to the right of the hat flew up and fell all round him and this was followed almost before the chips had started to fall by the sound of gunfire.

Karago was perhaps ten feet away and called back softly. "Again, do it again, but wait ten breaths. Keep doing it until he makes a hit."

But the man with the gun took the bait only once more. This time the bullet passed so close that it seemed to bore a hole in the air near enough to Quarshie's hat to have burned it but when he lowered it there was no mark on it. He was examining it carefully when he heard a gun fired over to his right and realised that Karago had found a position from which he could, perhaps, see his target.

With a tremendous exertion of will Quarshie resisted the temptation to look over the low parapet of rock which was protecting him.

Again Karago fired.

Quarshie squirmed around so that he could see Yosofo. The young man was lying on his side and his face looked like the map of a river delta, with blood replacing water.

Karago fired a third time and then, after a moment, called, "The man is leaving, *dono*. He has a lorry." To an African anything which was not a sedan, or other conventional private car, was a lorry.

Karago's gun cracked again and then, a few moments later, he knelt up from behind some rocks thirty or forty feet away and said, "The man there was wearing a white *bubu* and had a black face."

Quarshie had just remembered the French ambassador's statement that René, or as he had called him, André Grevier, was a "ver' good *chasseur* and champion with a carbine," and he had to revise the thought that the Frenchman might have been the one shooting at them with such deadly accuracy. Then he had to put any thoughts of the assassin out of his mind and attend to Yosofo.

One look told him that though he was not dead he was probably seriously injured. The bullet which had struck him had, as some military men say, "parted his hair." It had struck the very top of his skull causing concussion which might, or might not, lead to the impairment of his motor functions depending upon whether his skull and therefore his brain had been damaged and to what extent.

"Is he dead, *dono?*"

Quarshie shook his head. "It was a close thing." As he spoke he tore a large piece out of the white robe the young man was wearing and made a pad out of it. With another strip of cloth he tied the pad lightly on the top of his patient's head to stop the extensive bleeding.

"We will move him into the shade of that rock for a few moments," Quarshie told Karago, "while I look again at what I saw, there, where the woman was killed."

In the cleavage of the rock, where Martha had died and bled, Quarshie reached down almost the length of his arm and brought up two items. A small flat piece of rock painted with gilt and a very blood-soaked piece of paper on which there appeared to be some writing. He put his arm down again and this time came up with two more pieces of gilded rock. All three were roughly the same size and shape as the true pieces of gold that Mrs. Quarshie had found in Martha's hairbrush. He clawed down into the cleft for the third time but found nothing else.

"Gold, *dono?*" The hunter was standing just behind him.

"Somebody was meant to think so, old one."

"Bait in a trap?" Karago knew his trade, whether the hunt was for animals or men.

"Bait, my friend. Yes, bait and it caught the one it was meant for."

"The woman?"

"The woman. Today it nearly got me and may leave the young man here without the power of his arms and legs." A thought suddenly struck Quarshie. "And it would have gotten me, old one, if it had not been for you. You saved my life."

"Would that be worth the price of a new gun, *dono?* For if I had had one that man would never have got away."

"The best that money can buy, old man."

The journey back to the car tested Quarshie's strength to its limit. Yosofo was not heavy but to carry him so that his injury was not aggravated was a trial of patience and endurance.

The only way that he could be transported was pickaback but Quarshie had to carry him very high so that Yosofo's head rested on the doctor's shoulder. Karago walked beside them steadying the unconscious man's head and occasionally, standing back to back with Quarshie, lifting the young man's weight to give Quarshie a few minutes' rest.

There was no alternative to coping with their problem the way they did. If Quarshie, alone, had made the best time he could into Norenga and back with men and a stretcher and some kind of transport they probably would not have gotten Yosofo into hospital much before dawn the next day and could well have had to face the problem of carrying him across the difficult terrain in the dark.

As he moved doggedly towards the road Quarshie felt as if the boiling air was somewhere between solid and fluid and he had to fight his way through it like a swimmer loaded with lead weight. They had water bottles but it seemed as if, as he drank the water, his body became porous and the liquid passed right through the tissues of his flesh and out of his pores. Sweat dripped off his nose, his chin and his elbows and his shoes squelched as he walked as they would have if he had worn them to walk through a river.

The metal of the car, when they returned to it, was so hot that even Karago, when he leant against the bodywork in helping Quarshie to set down his load, recoiled with an exclamation.

Finally, with the hunter in the back cradling Yosofo's head to cushion him from unavoidable bumps . . . though Quarshie, tired as he was, did his best to avoid them . . . they started slowly back towards Norenga.

As he drove and he recovered a little from his physical exhaustion, Quarshie's mind started, from a state of fatigue-induced torpor, to come alive again. A great many events had taken place and they had to be set, like pieces in a jig-saw puzzle, into the picture he was trying to construct of Martha's death and the circumstances surrounding it.

First there was Yosofo. Probably the least that could be expected from his wound was a subdural hematoma, a kind of blood clot developing around the brain. That meant X rays and the services of a neurosurgeon. He would, therefore, have to be transported to Port St. Mary as soon as possible.

Next; what was next? The fact that they had been attacked. Had they been set up for the attack? Someone had known that they were going to be in the vicinity of the place where Martha had been murdered. Who? Who had known that they were going to be there? Only he, himself, Mrs. Quarshie and Yosofo. So the young man must have spoken of it. To whom and why? For the time being and possibly for weeks, or months, that could well be his secret. The fact that he had been shot meant nothing. If he had been a partner in a plot his confederate might have wanted to get rid of him in case he talked.

Or, and Quarshie tended to favour the thought, Yosofo had been the innocent victim of his own carelessness. If that was the case Quarshie felt only pity for him.

The would-be murderer had a black face and had worn a white *bubu*. Karago's words had been strange. "Black face."

"The man with the gun," he said over his shoulder, "you said he had a black face."

"Yes, *dono*."

"Would you say I had a black face, or that your brothers had black faces?"

"Neither you nor they are as black as that one."

Quarshie knew that he had started a line of thought, of reappraisal, in the old man's mind and waited to see what would come of it. The hunter's sight was still very keen and he was very observant.

Presently he said, "Your skin and mine, *dono,* even when we are not sweating, shines. The skin of that man did not shine, that is why it was so black."

Quarshie said, "That is most interesting. And the man's features?"

"I could not see them, *dono,* he was too far away. It seems though that the whites around his eyes were very large like those of a madman."

Quarshie pigeonholed that information in his memory along with what the hunter had said earlier and turned back a page or two in his mental file to the imitation gold and the piece of paper which sat forgotten in his pocket.

He pulled off the road.

To Karago he said, "I must stop for a moment to look at that piece of paper I found where the woman died."

He got out of the car and reached into his pocket, where his fingers found it. The paper, now, was not only bloodstained but sodden with his sweat. Carefully he pulled it out and, even more carefully, unfolded it. There was, or had been, something written on it but all he was able to decipher appeared to be clusters of letters or numerals. His perspiration and the bloodstains made it impossible to determine more than that.

He got back into the car and drove on.

CHAPTER TEN

"A man who is afraid of tree snakes will probably tread on a viper."

Quarshie dragged himself up the steep, interminable slope out of an exhausted sleep. His back and shoulder muscles ached and for a few moments he hated the thought of returning to the problems Martha's death created for him. There seemed to be no end to them.

Painfully he turned on his back and stared at the ceiling. He had transferred his responsibility for Yosofo to Levitsky. The young man had started to regain consciousness as they drove into Norenga but he had an insufferable headache which consumed him to the point where he was totally unaware of anything else.

Levitsky had examined him as well as he could, given the facilities he had, and had offered the opinion that it seemed unlikely that the young man's skull had been fractured though they would have to await the X-ray results to be quite sure. Arrangements would be made to transport him to Port St. Mary and with him the spade which had been discovered near Martha's grave. It was now encased in a plastic bag and before he went to bed Quarshie had listed the tests he wanted made on it at the understaffed and underequipped police laboratory. He had enclosed with it a copy of a brief report he had written for Jedawi in which, besides detailing the other facts of the case so far, he had emphasised the importance of the work that had to be done by the laboratory.

He had also directed that a copy of the report be sent "as a courtesy" to the local Norenga superintendent of police. In an aside to Mrs. Quarshie he had said, "For 'courtesy' read 'threat.' I have to treat the whole police force as an enemy because that is the way all those with senior rank treat me. In their local regions most of them, like this man here, have more power than the judiciary or the administration."

Then he had gone to bed.

Now it was a new day and he had to determine his next move in his search for Martha's murderer.

By instinct rather than logic he decided that he should make the first assault of the day on Ephraim. Obviously the D.O. knew more than he had told Quarshie at their first meeting.

With a sigh, as he dragged himself painfully to his feet, the doctor acknowledged that probably the same thing could be said for everyone in Norenga who had had anything to do with Martha, which could mean that they all had something to hide.

He had not told anyone about the piece of paper he had found soaked with Martha's blood, except Mrs. Quarshie. He had asked her to dry it out for him. It was on the dressing table and he was able to determine that what was written on it was made up of long and short blocks of still largely undecipherable numerals. He could, however, see quite clearly that it appeared to be a message written in some kind of numerical code.

When he called the rest-house steward to bring hot water so that he could wash, his wife came in from the verandah, where she had been sitting while she waited for him to wake up.

She was wide-eyed and troubled and her first words were, "You might have been dead now, Quarshie, and I might . . . I might have been a widow." This was the first sign of perturbation that she had shown since he had brought Yosofo into the hospital the previous evening but she had agonised over it all the time he had been sleeping.

During the hours immediately after his return she had tackled the practical issues, taking care of Karago, contacting Yosofo's relatives and helping Levitsky when he had had the young man on the operating table to examine him. Also she had had the steward get a bath for her husband and had, herself, prepared food for him and seen him into bed.

Quarshie put his arm around her and said, "But you are not a widow and I am not dead. What might have happened yesterday is only important if it is an indication of what might happen tomorrow."

"Yes, Quarshie, I know, but you have to be careful."

"More careful than I was yesterday, certainly. But a man

who is afraid of tree snakes will probably tread on a viper. It is very difficult to look in all directions at once and if I do that I may be so busy being defensive that I may miss a chance to find some truth, or fact, that will get rid of both the tree snakes and the vipers."

"Well if you are going to do any more seeking for the truth like you did yesterday I am going to be with you. Man should have been born with four eyes instead of two, then he could watch all around him at the same time. But tomorrow you will have your eyes and my eyes."

"Two targets instead of one."

Mrs. Quarshie shrugged. "Then that's the way it will have to be."

"And what about your work for Levitsky? You were with him all day today?"

"I was, but if I were not here he would manage. Now, where are we going to start?"

Quarshie said, "So, Mr. District Officer, I thought you had better have a firsthand report of what happened yesterday, particularly with regard to the discovery of that shovel, so that you could include it in your file on Martha."

Ephraim said sourly, "The superintendent has already been in and shown me a copy of your report to Jedawi. He is talking of resigning."

"Would that be a bad thing?"

Ephraim shrugged. "I don't know. In fact I don't know anything anymore. Though if you go out, without police protection, and get yourself killed, I'm the one who will get the blame because the superintendent says he has washed his hands of you."

"Precisely. The police are hardly very co-operative."

"I can't do anything about that."

"I know."

"What do you mean, you know?"

Quarshie said, "When I talked with the superintendent the

first time I saw him he said that you set the people a bad example and made his work more difficult for him."

"He's a bastard."

"What was he talking about?"

"You're a bastard, too, Sam. You get everybody unnecessarily stirred up." Then he tried to make a joke of his condemnation by turning to Mrs. Quarshie and asking, "You would have to admit, wouldn't you, Prudence, that he is a bit of a bastard sometimes? That's why he was a good boxer. He never missed an opening when someone offered him one. He hit 'em, and there was a couple of hundred pounds behind every punch. He used to win most of his fights with a knockout."

Mrs. Quarshie made a mental note to ask Quarshie what had changed him from being an aggressive pugilist into a man who went out of his way to avoid violence. To Ephraim she said, "He is good at finishing anything he starts."

"All right. I'll qualify my statement and say that he is a determined bastard. And to answer your question, Sam, the superintendent dislikes me because I once pulled rank on a couple of his subordinates who thought they had caught Martha doing a little smuggling. She was coming into town on one of the roads the smugglers use. She had no right to be there but neither had they any right to arrest her without having evidence that she was up to something illegal."

"What was she up to?"

"She wouldn't tell me."

"And why were you meeting her?"

"Shall we call it a lovers' tryst?"

"I didn't ask what you might call it, I asked 'Why?'"

Ephraim shrugged irritably. "O.K. From the point where we were to meet there is a track to her bungalow which cuts out going through the town. She was getting sensitive about the gossip we provoked when people saw us together."

"Where does that road the smugglers use lead to?"

"To a point on the frontier."

There was a map of Ephraim's district on the wall behind him.

"Can you show me the exact location of the road?"

Ephraim turned in his chair and ran his finger up the map.

Quarshie crossed the room, studied it carefully, then returned to his chair and said slowly, "I see. Now, one more question, Ephraim, and we'll leave you alone. Did she ever talk to you about, or did she ever show you, anything that she had written in numerical code?"

"I saw something, two whole sheets of paper, lying on her desk and I thought first of all that she had been working out some kind of tables or something and I asked her what it was. She said she sent the important parts of the stories she wrote back to her editor in code because she didn't want nosy people at the office to know what she was up to. She obviously did not want me to press the point so I made no more reference to it."

Quarshie looked at him with a frown and said, "I hope you are telling me not just the truth but all of it. If there are any bits that you are leaving out, take care. The man who goes to build a bridge and ignores the strength of the current in the river is more likely to fail than to succeed."

In the car Mrs. Quarshie said, "I can understand why you may seem to be a determined bastard to some people but not what made you give up hitting people with a couple of hundred pounds behind each punch."

"The answer is simple. Worthwhile people don't give in because they've been punched, they just back off and come back at you some other way. The ones who aren't worthwhile and who give in save up their resentment until they can get back at you with a knife between the shoulder blades. Boxing is a game with fixed rules, but there are no rules for people's behaviour outside the ring. One kind of violence usually breeds a different kind and before you know where you are the whole thing has gone out of control." He glanced at his wife. "O.K.?"

"No. I thought the answer would be . . . more satisfying than that."

"Sometimes, with some people, it may be. Sometimes a man feels he should behave kindly to those who are weaker than he is by showing mercy or pity or something, is that what you mean?"

They were heading out of town and Mrs. Quarshie, feeling that there was no point in pursuing her line of questioning any further, switched direction. "Where are we going?" she asked.

"Mama Anoma. She asked me to take you out to see her, remember?"

"That's nice. But what is the real reason?"

"To find out where Martha had been before she met Ephraim. I am almost sure she would not have been on that road because she was smuggling. It must lead to some other place besides the frontier. Besides, I have an obligation to call on Anoma because one of her family got hurt when he was with me."

"I thought you said that Yosofo had had to act as interpreter."

"Linguist would have been more exact." Usually, in Africa, it is impossible to address a tribal chief directly. Everything that is said to him has to pass through a third person, a linguist. It is a method of underlining the chief's status and it allows him, because he will usually understand perfectly what is being said to him by his petitioner or whoever it is who is addressing him, time to consider his answer.

"Anoma certainly speaks Hausa many times better than I do. Now that we have established the relationship I am going to insist that we speak as equals. I don't think she will have any objection."

In this assumption Quarshie was correct, though he and Mrs. Quarshie were forced to wait for almost an hour while the old lady prepared herself for the meeting. Though what she had to prepare since she wore somewhat less than the equivalent of a Western bikini and had no furniture in her hut was hard to determine.

After they had waited in the "greeting" room of the compound until it suited Anoma to see them they were fetched by a pert but very respectful little girl who was obviously the day's attendant on the woman who was probably her great-grand-mother.

Quarshie greeted Anoma according to protocol and she followed through the ritual litany the way most people repeat litanies, with her mind on something else. In fact, she was studying Mrs. Quarshie. When the regular overture was at an end and Quarshie had commiserated with her and her family on the injuries Yosofo had suffered, she thanked him and said, "So this is your clever woman. You are welcome, daughter. It is said, big man, that the mango tree which produces the most beautiful flowers never produces the best fruit . . . but in this one both fruit and flower are surely perfect."

It was a graceful compliment and Mrs. Quarshie replied, "Mother, the honour of being your daughter also makes me your most willing servant."

Quarshie thought that the instant allegiance that appeared to have come into being between the two women created what could be a formidable force.

Anoma accepted Mrs. Quarshie's homage with a slight inclination of her head and turned to Quarshie and asked, "What brings you back so soon, big man, and without warning?"

"Mother, in a hunt for evil men, it is like trying to catch a rat, a moment's hesitation and the creature can turn the delay into distance and therefore into escape. So there is little time for good manners. For this I ask you forgiveness."

"I understand," Anoma said. "What help can I give you?"

"I need to know some details about one of the roads used by the smugglers."

"You think I know so much of them?"

"Let us say that you know people who know so much of them and I need you to direct me to such a person."

"It is one particular road you wish to know about?"

"It is and it leaves the main road towards the evening sun a little the other side of the bridge over the river."

"What is your interest in it?"

"It goes, like all such roads, to the frontier. I wish to know where else it goes."

"Why do you think it goes somewhere else?"

"The white woman who was killed used it, and she had no cause to smuggle."

Anoma sat with the kind of stillness that can be observed only in people who are much practiced in meditation and she retained her pose for so long that Mrs. Quarshie wondered whether, perhaps, it had some connection with the age of her mind and its inability to flow freely.

At last she said, "I have looked at all I know of that road and there is one who has trusted me and whom I will entrust to you. She came to me for protection, which I willingly gave her. She must, herself, decide how much she will help you." And she spoke softly to her little attendant, saying, "Fetch me Kumba, child."

A few minutes later they were joined by a striking woman and the Quarshies knew that from her high cheekbones and sharp, almost aquiline nose that she was of the Malinke people, who have a rich musical heritage and play a complicated, twenty-one string lute called a *kora*. She was of the same people who had been, before Columbus visited America, amongst those who led the world in the discovery and export of gold and ornaments made of that material. And nobody needed to tell the Quarshies that she was a walk-about girl. It was apparent in the way she carried herself and regarded them when she returned their examination of her.

Anoma held a rapid conversation with her for a few moments in a language that was unknown to Quarshie. Then the old lady spoke in Hausa.

"Kumba will guide you, big man, she will also tell you something that is widely known but never spoken of because the information carries with it a heavy load of fear for all who know of it or speak of it. Do not betray that trust for if you do many may suffer and the load will rest on my old shoulders. Take Kumba, who will hide her face while she is in public, and go well, my son, and you too, my daughter. If you succeed in doing what you will find you have to do, you will earn the gratitude of every woman in Norenga and for many miles around here but you must be careful; behind those who show on their faces and in their manner that they are helping you there will be men who live only to do harm to women and to those who come between them and their quarry."

Kumba, when she came into Anoma's hut, had been wearing a richly patterned batik cloth. When she joined the Quarshies in their car she had changed into the plain blue cloth, with a veil, usually worn by Tuaregs. This permitted her to hide her features completely, leaving only a slit through which she could see.

She sat silent in the front seat beside Quarshie until they reached the rest house. There, once the louvred windows had been closed, she lowered the veil and sat boldly at her ease in the chair which Quarshie had pushed forward for her. After looking from Quarshie to Mrs. Quarshie and back to the doctor she said, *"Dono,* I know you are an important man. Your lady, too, is important but I am not afraid of important people. Men are men. Some talk more, some talk less. Some have big muscles, some have almost no muscles at all. Every one of them asks me for the same thing and so long as they pay the price I give them what they want.

"What you are going to ask for is different because it is what I want also—that is an end to women being used by men when and how they will and not paying any price for it."

Quarshie said, "I see and I shall be glad of your help." He was not, however, at all sure that he knew what she was talking about. "It would help my understanding and my ability to plan my actions if you would first answer some questions."

"Anything you ask, *dono.*"

"What is happening to the walk-about women that makes Anoma and you speak of women being ill-used by men?"

"Not just ill-used, *dono.* In my trade being ill-used is not uncommon and has its price so that she who sells herself and knows what to expect can make some profit from what she has to suffer. No, what is happening is that others are actually taking their freedom and getting, many times over, the bride price which had already been lost to the women's fathers when they joined this trade. *Dono,* it is well known and accepted every-

where that 'nothing goes for nothing,' but here the new rule is
that 'everything goes for nothing.'"

Mrs. Quarshie thought she knew what Kumba was talking
about.

Attitudes to prostitution in Africa vary from tribe to tribe. In
most of the big cities the profession is looked upon as a way of
earning a living, though acceptance of the institution is more
complicated than it appears on the surface. For instance, in
Port St. Mary and some other big towns, women from certain
northern tribes are virtually all divorcees and they buy or rent
houses in the *zongo,* where they lodge and sell food to passing
strangers. They also have visitors who come to talk and to listen to music as well as to avail themselves of the other services
the women offer. Often the women fulfill a contract on a
weekly, or even monthly, basis for what amounts to the satisfaction of all the care and needs that are common to men who
are homeless and living amongst strangers.

The women whom Mrs. Quarshie knew best, through her
work as midwife and general counsellor on women's problems,
were those who were known as *tutu* girls, a name which had
originated in the old days when it was the custom for women to
declare their prices before they could expect their customers to
accept their services. At that time the common price had always
been "two benis, two benis," hence the two, two, or *tutu.*

There was one feature which was, however, common to all
the prostitutes whom Mrs. Quarshie knew. They owned themselves and refused to work for, or share their earnings with, any
kind of a proprietor. So, she thought that it was some kind of
forced proprietorship that Kumba was talking about, but she
was wrong. It was something much worse.

"*Dono,* the girls are not selling themselves anymore,"
Kumba explained. "They are being sold by others, taken to
market and sold like slaves."

"Who is taking them, how are they sold and to whom?"

"The new chief and the white man with pictures on his arms
are the traders. Those whom they steal are taken across the
frontier and it is said that those who buy them are men from
Libya where there is a mad king who believes that all who do

not share his narrow belief in Islam should serve those who do."

"How do you know all this and why have you not spoken to someone in authority of it?"

"I was taken myself, *dono,* but I escaped. That is how I know. As for speaking to someone in authority, I do not believe that there is anyone here who would listen. Indeed, I believe that all such men are paid to stop their ears to such things as I could tell them. But I spoke with that white woman. When she was killed I became afraid that they would kill me, too."

"Why, since you escaped, have you not run back to your own country?"

"Because they have a little girl I took with me, *dono.* She is twelve. They look for children of her age. I have been seeking a way to save her. It is why I am here speaking to you."

"You know where this place is?"

"I do. The road you spoke of to Anoma leads to it."

"But how do they get the girls? How did they get you to go to this place?"

"It is simple. First, the young chief invited me to go to his house. He paid me well. Later he invited me again and told me to bring a younger girl with me. Then he took us both to that place there along the road you spoke of. There we were put in chains."

"How did you escape?"

"The white man fancied me himself. He was careless. I escaped while he and the others slept. It was not difficult. Though it was hard to walk from there to here without following that track, the one you were speaking of."

"Will you take me to this place?"

"We shall go in your car?"

"Certainly."

"Then I will show you the place but I will wait outside with your car."

"You are afraid to go in even though I and Mrs. Quarshie will be with you?"

"I am."

It was said simply and without hesitation.

CHAPTER ELEVEN

"When you speak of guns to me, cock, you're speaking wiv a man wot understands 'em."

Shirley's compound looked like a military block house and fitted into its rocky surroundings as snugly as a keystone fits into an arch. It was obviously the work of a man with access to building supplies, especially concrete, which were not commonly available in the region.

The structure made use of its surrounding rocks for its walls, with cement poured into the interstices to make them more or less continuous. The result, as the Quarshies discovered later, was to create rooms of very irregular and intriguing shapes.

The place stood at the end of a turning off the track along which Kumba had guided them from Norenga. The entrance was through a short gorge with steep rocky façades on each side.

Quarshie parked his car out of sight of the house and, leaving Kumba in it, he and Mrs. Quarshie walked up the paved surface through the construction man's private canyon.

"It's cold, hard and brutal," Mrs. Quarshie said, "frightening." And she took her husband's hand.

At the end of the defile they came to the wide face of concrete which tied the rocks, on either side, together. In the middle there was a small, heavy door, made of planks of highly polished ebony heartwood.

Incongruously the door was fitted with a massive brass knocker, which, like the door, glittered in the last of the evening sunlight. When Quarshie used it the sound resembled the one made by the great hollowed tree trunks called, by the people where Quarshie came from, talking drums.

It was Shirley Temple himself who answered the door. He was wearing a pale-blue satin *baba riga,* a kind of smock which fell from the neck and shoulders in many, many folds and was embroidered from the collar down over his chest with gold thread in an intricate design of arabesques.

He was surprised, and peering at Quarshie, who was standing against the light, he said, " 'Ullo, 'ullo . . . 'oo do we 'ave here? Why, if it ain't the great man 'imself, Dr. Quarshie and 'is ever so lovely wife. I am flattered, reely I am. Come in, come in. And 'ow did you find your way to this little 'ideaway of mine, then?"

"We have a mutual friend, Mr. Temple . . ."

"Mr. Temple! 'Oo is Mr. Temple? I ain't 'eard of anyone 'ere wiv that name in ever such a long time. Though there is someone called Shirley, or sometimes by 'is hinferiors, Mr. Shirley. So, if you please, it's Shirley and then we shall know 'oo you are talking to. And we 'ave a mutual friend, eh? Now 'oo would that be? Sol Levitsky? Or Percy? Or Ephraim?"

"They all know that you live here? I thought this hideaway, as you call it, and its location was a secret."

"But not from me friends, mate. A man 'as to 'ave one or two of them 'oo can come calling on 'im, now doesn't 'ee?"

As he spoke Shirley led them through a dark hallway into a wide courtyard that had a baobab tree in the centre of it.

There he paused, evidently by habit, to savour the effect the scene had on his visitors, for not only was there the dramatic shape of the tree but, unlike the outside of his residence, the walls on the inside were a brilliant patchwork of colour with the floor of the courtyard and the surfaces surrounding it covered with multicoloured Moroccan tiles.

"You see, Doc," he said after they had had time to take it all in, "we are all of us, up 'ere, heccentrics, Levitsky, Percy, that frog René and me. Why would we be 'ere if we weren't, eh? This place is one of my heccentricities. That old tree there in the middle was wot made me build 'ere. *Hadansonia digitata* the professors call it. She's beautiful and I fell in love with 'er the first time I saw 'er. I thought, if she can live 'ere, so can I. And 'ere we are." Then, as if he had suddenly remembered something, he added, " 'Ere, there's a skelington inside 'er. You want to see it? There when I found it, it was. I always 'eard they used to stick corpses in the 'ollows of these trees. I don't know 'ow long 'ee's been in there. Sol Levitsky told me it was

the skelington of a man, or else I wouldn't 'ave known." He
pointed. "I call 'im Joshua. Go on Mrs.," Shirley said, " 'ave a
look. 'Ee won't bite you. Leastways, 'ee's never bitten anyone
yet." And then to Quarshie: "But she's a beauty, my *hadansonia,* ain't she? Took me tape measure to 'er the other day to
see 'ow much she's growed. Forty-two feet around the trunk
she was when I found 'er. Fifty-one she is now. For me it's like
'aving a woman in the 'ouse you know. Talk to 'er, I do, tell 'er
all me secrets and troubles. Between you an' me, Doc, women
don't 'ave no savvy for the kind of things I tell 'er. Only good
for one thing they are." Then, as Mrs. Quarshie came back, he
turned his attention and his flood of words towards her. "When
I 'and in me dinner pail I expect to join 'im. That's wot I've
told my people to do with me. You see . . ." He paused. "I do
carry on, don't I? I must shut me face or I'll be telling you all
the secrets I tell 'er and that would never do. 'Ere, come over
'ere, sit down and I'll get some beer. Isn't every day I 'ave
guests. Maggie," he shouted, and when a woman came he spoke
a few words to her in a language the Quarshies didn't understand. "It's African beer"—he was speaking again to the doctor—"lovely stuff. Maggie makes it. She's not much use for anything else, now. The old trouble and strife . . . that's wot they
used to call their women in East 'Am, where I come from. But
she keeps the place clean and cooks and . . ."

He was about to say something else but thought better of it.

"So why 'ave you come to see me, eh, Doc? It's not just a social visit, I'm sure of that. Got something to do wiv the late
unlamented Martha, 'as it?"

"You didn't like her?"

" 'Oo did? Proper Nosy Parker she was. Always poking
around in everybody else's business."

"You mean she was interested in construction work?"

"Come off it, Doc. You've got more nous than that. She only
wanted to know the kind of things that people don't talk about,
like wot the Jerries did to poor 'Anna. Or why Percy was cut
off wiv-hout a bob by 'is haristocratic and noble family. Skel-
ingtons in the cupboard, that's wot she was hinterested hin.

When she came 'ere I showed 'er old Joshua. I didn't tell 'er wot I was goin' to show 'er. Jus' took 'er and let 'er put 'er long nose in there. And I fixed it so that she came face to face with 'im." He laughed. "I thought she was goin' to 'ave forty fits."

The woman brought the beer in a large bowl made from a gourd and three china mugs. She set them down in the shade of a roofed corner of the courtyard where the Quarshies and Shirley had settled on big, overstuffed cushion-like mattresses. After a word or two to Shirley in her own language she departed.

"Go on, Mrs., dig in. It's lovely stuff." Shirley scooped a mugful of the cloudy liquid out of the gourd for himself. "And you still 'aven't told me 'oo our mutual friend is 'oo showed you the way 'ere."

"Her name is Kumba."

Shirley paused fractionally in the movement he was making to bring his mug to his mouth, then continued with it and drank deeply. As he lowered the mug he said, "Oh, 'er. And wot kind of story 'as she been telling you? None of the girls wot young Montague, 'ee's the young chief you know and Montague ain't 'is real name it's only wot I call 'im, none of the girls 'ee brings up 'ere understands properly wot is goin' on."

"What is going on, Shirley?"

"Well now, Doc, that's something I am not at liberty to tell you. You know 'ow it is. Some things is out in the open growing up fine and loverly under Gawd's blue and beautiful sky and some things, like roots, 'as to stay in the dark."

"What about murder and black slaving, Shirley?"

"Wot about 'em? You tell me."

"A woman who found out rather a lot about the local girls who have been disappearing came to a nasty sticky end the other day."

"So?"

"I've been sent up here to investigate both black slaving and murder, and the trail has led me here, not to look at your baobab tree but to ask you what you know about the killing of the American woman and the disappearance of the girls."

"Well that's a plain enough question, ain't it? And if I told you to go and screw yourself, Doc, wot would your answer be to that?"

"I would take it as an admission of guilt and insist that you be put under arrest."

"And 'oo do you expect would do a nasty unfriendly thing like that to poor old Shirley, eh?"

"Certainly not your friend the police superintendent. But there are other ways to ensure that those who break the law are put on trial. In this country a verdict which says that a man is guilty of murder means a firing squad."

"Oh . . . so it's guns is it? Well, do you know wot my answer is to that, Doc?" He had his right hand inside his *baba riga.* "This." His hand came out from beneath his robe holding a heavy, old-fashioned Luger pistol. "When you speak of guns to me, cock, you're speaking wiv a man wot understands 'em. They tell me you are a clever man 'oo can talk English and French and quite a few African lingos. Wot language do you use when you speak with this little 'andful? And don't move, Mrs., unless you want me to poke a hole or two in your big and 'andsome 'ubby." He got up and moved towards Quarshie, pushing the barrel of the gun into his face. "Now, talk clever, mate, because I can end your talking days by squeezing this 'ere trigger ever such a little bit."

Quarshie said quietly, "There are quite a lot of people who know I am here, a couple of them are waiting in the car outside, so you won't get away with anything. They are in direct radio contact with the army."

Shirley laughed. "You don't fool me, mate. I sent Maggie to look when she went for the beer. That's why she took so long. An empty car was all she saw. And as for your friends in the army I'm not so green as I'm cabbage-looking. I didn't build this place with only one way in and out. That was 'ow that black bitch Kumba got away. She found wot you might call the back door." Mrs. Quarshie, praying that she was doing the right thing, stood up suddenly. For a fraction of a second Shirley's attention was distracted from Quarshie. With his left hand the doctor jerked Shirley's fist with the gun in it up towards the roof. At the same time he planted a savage short-arm blow in the man's solar plexus, and then, as his head came forward, Quarshie brought his right fist up under Shirley's jaw with all the two-hundred-pound force that Ephraim had claimed he could bring into action.

Shirley's head whipped back as if the strings which held it to his body had snapped. Almost before his shoulder blades reached the floor Quarshie was standing over him. Shirley did not move.

Quarshie took a deep breath and said, "You were very clever, Prudence. I'm not so sure I was. I may have killed him." He spaced the last five words out with pauses between them. "And that won't help. Never mind, if he's still alive I'll tie him up and then take a look around. Go and corner Maggie while I take care of this object." He indicated Shirley and flexed the fingers of his right hand with his left. "I have cracked some of my knuckles on his jaw."

As Mrs. Quarshie went to find the woman, Quarshie knelt beside Shirley, raised one of his eyelids and leant forward and put his ear on the unconscious man's chest to check his heart. Then, with his undamaged hand, he felt gently around Shirley's jaw. As he did so he remembered one of his professors in medical school saying, "The modern human mandible is a poor thing in comparison with that of creatures who are much lower on the scale of evolutionary development." He had apparently proved the professor's statement to be correct because he detected a fracture of the temporo-mandibular joints. Quarshie shrugged and thought that in the end it would be the least of Shirley's injuries if he could establish that the man had killed Martha, though, as yet, he had no positive evidence to link him with the crime. Tearing panels of cloth out of his *baba riga,* Quarshie strapped the man's jaw roughly in place, immobilising it. Then he tied his wrists and ankles together.

Mrs. Quarshie came back with the woman and said, "I can't make her understand a word. I think she speaks Hausa."

Maggie had been in her room, apparently unaware of what had been taking place.

Quarshie told her and she listened stony-faced. When he had finished she said, "He knew it would happen one day, *dono*. He had expected it to happen before. What are you going to do with him?"

"I am going to take him to Port St. Mary. You will come with him."

"Now?"

"Now."

"Will you give me a little moment to prepare?"

"Were the women ever given time to prepare?"

"*Dono,* I had nothing to do with the women except feed them."

"Were there a great number?"

"There were."

"How many?"

"*Dono,* I did not count. There is a room with mats in it. You can count them. About once each moon, when all the mats were filled, they would be taken away."

"Who brought the women here?"

"Various men. I did not know them."

"Did a white woman come here?"

"A fat one?"

Quarshie nodded.

"She did."

"Did she leave here alive?"

"He never killed anyone."

"Are you sure?"

The woman thought for a moment and then amended her statement. "He never killed anyone who came here to this house, or to any house that I shared with him. Nor did he ever speak of having killed anyone."

"What is your true name?"

"My mother called me Anja."

"Is there anyone else in this place, Anja?"

"No one, *dono*."

"And all the rooms are open?"

"They are."

To his wife Quarshie said, "Stay with her and call me if you need help. I am going to look around. Anja, prepare yourself to leave."

Apart from the quaint shape of some of the rooms, which was only of passing interest to him, the most important thing Quarshie found was the cell with the sleeping mats in it. Beside the mats there were rings embedded in the concrete walls with chains attached to them. At their free ends the chains had bracelets with padlocks on them.

In the room next door, which appeared to be the one Shirley had inhabited, the most striking thing was its orderliness. Its contents fitted it according to an exact plan and its dominant feature was a cleverly arranged display of erotic wood carvings. In another room Quarshie found a bench, tools and a half-finished piece of sculpture which suggested that Shirley made the carvings himself and might have been a better than average sculptor had his interest been in the quality of what he was producing rather than its eroticism.

When he returned to Mrs. Quarshie and Anja he was absent-mindedly nursing his right hand, which was beginning to swell.

Mrs. Quarshie took one look at it, found a kerosene-powered refrigerator and insisted on applying crushed ice to the hand and then bandaging it firmly with torn-up strips of cloth.

Shirley recovered consciousness long before they were half-way back to Norenga. He was in the back of the car, with Anja, a very unhappy and uncomfortable man with his hands tied behind him and a broken jaw. He sat on the outside of the seat, with Anja next to him and Kumba beside her. The latter had hidden amongst the rocks until the Quarshies had reappeared.

Shirley whined when he spoke and had to produce his words without moving his jaw. Mrs. Quarshie was driving and Quarshie was twisted around in the front seat beside her so that he could keep an eye on his prisoner.

"'Ave a 'eart, mate," Shirley moaned. "Wot 'arm did I ever do to you?"

Quarshie did not reply. He was grimmer and more sombre than usual. His eyelids drooped to the point where his eyes were almost hidden and he shut out the sound of Shirley's complaints, concentrating totally on his thoughts.

Kumba's expression was as bleak as Quarshie's. The girl she had wanted to save was gone and it gave her no satisfaction that the man responsible was Quarshie's prisoner for it would not bring the girl back. A similar thought was in Quarshie's mind when he spoke across Shirley's drizzle of words and said, "There are a couple of questions you are going to have to answer either when I ask them or when someone else asks them, someone who will be far more inclined to beat you to get answers than I am. First, where are the girls you shipped out? And then, who else is involved in this foul traffic?"

"I don't know. I don't know where they are. You'll have to ask that friggin' Frog. 'Ee set it all up. 'Ee got me into it."

"And I suppose he made all the profits from it."

"Oh, I made my bit, of course I did, but it wasn't anything to write 'ome about. 'Ee did the marketing, see? So I don't know 'ow much 'ee ever got for them. Wot are you going to do with me and Anja? She never done nothing except make food for 'em and look after 'em a bit."

Quarshie said, "I'll remember that." But did not answer Shirley's question because he did not make up his mind until they were entering the outskirts of Norenga. Then, in the coast language which was Mrs. Quarshie's mother tongue, he said, "We'll drop Kumba at Anoma's compound, then we will drive straight through to Port St. Mary. I shall be able to take spells with you on the way down. It's only just after eight, now. If we drive hard we should be there before Jedawi goes into his morning cabinet meeting."

Mrs. Quarshie said nothing for a long time while Quarshie waited patiently for her reaction. When it came it surprised him, as her comments frequently did, because her words so often seemed to bear no relation to the subject they were discussing. She said, "Sam," a name she used only on very special occasions, "you were marvellous."

Quarshie looked puzzled.

"Yes, marvellous. Now I know what Ephraim meant when he said that in a fight you never missed an opening when someone offered you one." Then she added as an afterthought: "It might have been better for Shirley if he had heard him say it, too."

CHAPTER TWELVE

". . . the pleasures of concupiscence . . ."

Quarshie was driving, mainly with his left hand. The car was on a blacktop highway and did not need the effort that Mrs. Quarshie had had to put into holding it on the road over unpaved laterite surfaces. She was dozing, at the moment, beside him while Shirley whimpered softly in the back with his head on Anja's shoulder. Just after they had left Norenga, Quarshie had given him a shot of morphine, and the doctor thought that the man's distress was more an expression of his mental condition than his physical one.

It had been light since just after six and a look at his watch told the doctor that it was now almost nine. They had made good time and were beginning to enter the outskirts of Port St. Mary.

Ahead, against a bright, cloudless blue sky, the city shaped up as a sprawling conglomeration of forms that looked as if they had been put together by an ambitious child with a great pile of building blocks, a child who was determined to construct a metropolis like those he had seen in picture books of the large cities of Europe and America. The space in which he had to build—in this case, an almost unlimited area of Africa—was unimportant because, as he could see his models, everything had to go up into the sky. Of course the scale of his construction differed from his models. It had to because he had only toy bricks, a fact, however, which did not stop him from trying to express as extravagantly as he could his newly acquired conviction that height made might.

Brainwashed, Quarshie thought, blank mindlessness. Infantile imitation which disregards the real needs of the population and the culture for which the surroundings are supposed to provide a healthy background. What he was looking at he saw as an excrescence which had appeared on the land like an infection imported by outsiders, a contagion like the tuberculosis

and venereal disease that had also been introduced by the colo-
nists.

The buildings were supposed to be prestigious. In fact they
demeaned their surroundings and were hopelessly impractical
because the slabs of glass and concrete of which they were built
either baked those inside them or gulped expensive energy for
the air conditioning to keep them cool.

Quarshie sighed and reminded himself, irritably, not to get
worked up about things over which he had no control.

He was tired and his thirst kept reminding him of the beer in
the refrigerator in his house. It was a memory which, finally,
prompted him to change his plans. Instead of going directly to
see the President, he would, he decided, call in on his uncle, the
permanent secretary at the Ministry of Internal Affairs. In the
corridor outside the old man's office, beside the rows of filing
cabinets, there was a locked refrigerator full of beer and other
cold drinks and the key was on the perm sec's key ring.

The more he thought of the refrigerator the more Quarshie
found his change of plan appropriate. If his uncle's boss, the
minister, Major Obruensi, was there he could do all the business he needed to do with him and then allow the major to
make the required reports to Jedawi and the ambassador.

Since the police superintendent in Norenga was antagonistic
he was going to have to find some way around that problem, especially if he could get conclusive evidence out of Shirley that
would enable him to make a case against the Frenchman, René.
Obruensi was the man who could, and probably would, au-
thorise the dispatch of the reinforcements he was going to need.

Besides, the injury he had done to his hand was troubling
him. He wanted to get it X-rayed and put in a cast. Hand injuries were serious for a surgeon. He suspected that he had fractured or cracked the knuckle end of a metacarpal. If people
only knew, Quarshie thought, the amount of damage a knockout
punch with a bare fist did to the man delivering the punch, the
books and films that made a feature of violent fistfights would
be treated with the contempt they deserved.

At the same time he got his hand fixed he could have Shirley

put under guard and taken to an orthopedist to have his fractured jaw reduced. The man was in for a bad time in many
ways and Quarshie wondered whether he deserved, or would
get, any pity. He decided that it was a measure of a man's character whether he could ever be totally pitiless. There was always some quality, even in the worst criminals, which could
make them deserving of sympathy for their suffering. In Shirley's case, for instance, his thought for Maggie and his effort to
protect her from prosecution as an accomplice gave him some
right to be regarded as something less than a total villain.

Fifteen minutes later a military guard from the squad on
duty at the guard house in front of the ministry had been posted
to the car containing Shirley and his wife, and the Quarshies,
dusty and dishevelled, were sitting upstairs in the air-conditioned comfort of the perm sec's office. A moment or two later
the doctor had a glass of cold beer in his left hand and he
slowly emptied and refilled it twice before he was prepared to
go beyond presenting the very briefest greetings to his uncle.

So it was Mrs. Quarshie who started, in response to the old
man's enquiry, "So what have you two been up to?" to tell their
story. She gave a very concise account of their activities but,
along with answers to the perm sec's occasional questions, it
still took her a full ten minutes.

At the end the perm sec nodded and asked, "So what are
your priorities, now?" He was speaking to Quarshie.

"First, for someone to take over from the police superintendent. I suspect he is up to his ears in what has been going on
up in Norenga. In fact, it might be a good thing if the military
moved in and took charge for a while. When they arrive, which
should be as soon as possible, they should take the Frenchman,
the young chief and the superintendent into custody, on suspicion of being involved in black slaving."

"What about the woman, the American? What shall we be
able to tell her ambassador?"

"That we are making progress."

"Are you?"

"Off the record, yes, but I don't want to go into details yet."

"Do you know who killed her?"

"I think so, but I'm not sure."

"What else do you need?"

"I want to take the Englishman, Shirley, to hospital to get his jaw attended to and he should be under a twenty-four-hour guard all the time. When he is judged well enough, give him a pencil and paper and have him interrogated. He won't be able to move more than his lips for quite some time so it may be easier for him to write his answers. Have his woman interrogated separately. And, most important, I want their arrest kept a secret until you hear from me. That will be in two or three days. Finally, I want a good driver. The army will, I hope, airlift their mob up right away. I need time to get my hand fixed, to take a bath and to have a good night's sleep in my own bed. Then I will start back again but with someone else behind the wheel of the car."

The perm sec glanced down the notes he had been making. "And the President?"

"Write him one of your masterly reports in triplicate and have the minister deliver it as a matter of routine, tomorrow, after we are on our way back to Norenga."

"None of that sounds impossible. Wait, while I talk to the minister."

As the perm sec left the room Mrs. Quarshie said, "The most important items on your list are that we get your hand properly attended to and that we get to have a rest. Do you really know who killed Martha?"

"I can only repeat what I told the old man, that I think I do. But I have got to be sure."

"Dupré?"

Quarshie smiled. "Or Ephraim, or the superintendent, or Shirley . . . they all had motives. And even Percy may have had one. The fetisher certainly did and one has to suspect those two young Americans who admit to being in the neighbourhood at the time." His smile broadened. "Even Sol Levitsky is not totally above suspicion. So far, though, I am working on instinct rather than evidence."

"You really believe that one of them could have committed that brutal murder?"

Quarshie nodded. "Some could have done it in cold blood, others in a blind rage. She was an abrasive woman."

The perm sec put his head around the door and said, "The minister would like to see you."

As the Quarshies sat down in front of Obruensi the major said, "Sounds like you are having quite a jolly time, eh, Doctor?" Major Obruensi had spent several years at Sandhurst Military College in England and had acquired an exaggeratedly "British" manner of speech and attitude. Mrs. Quarshie noticed that he had also had someone manicure and polish his fingernails. "Frightful place, Norenga. Absolute end of the earth. Now, Doctor, your uncle has told me what you want and we will follow your instructions to the letter. That man you have in the car had a gun and threatened you with it, right?"

"Yes."

"Then that will take care of him until you can produce more conclusive evidence on his other activities. We can hold him almost indefinitely on a charge of illegal possession of firearms. You have the gun?"

"I do. I'll hand it over. It's locked in the back of the car."

"Nasty things, guns, what? Need to be trained how to handle them. Now . . . ah, the other thing I wanted to speak to you about is the man I propose to send to Norenga to relieve the police chappie of his duties. Do you remember Captain Iyrini? We put him in charge at the airport when we took over from the civilians a couple of years ago. You worked with him then."

Quarshie remembered him well. Iyrini was a very cool, professional young officer.

Obruensi asked, "Pretty capable young man, wouldn't you say?"

"He most certainly is."

"Good. Thought you would approve. Just wanted to be sure. Important to have the right men on your team, eh? He knows the district, too. A follower of Islam. We'll airlift him up there with a full company. Make it a military exercise. Keep our fellows on their toes. Actually, the President has given me orders to weed out a few of these police types who have built themselves empires. I'll have Iyrini on his way by noon, or soon afterwards. Leave any instructions you have for him with your uncle. Then there's the question of a driver. I have another old chum of yours on my staff. He's Sergeant Major, now, Ikwasti Johnson. Make a very efficient unit, the three of you. Was there anything else?"

The perm sec said, "We have put a guard around the clock on the Englishman while he is in hospital and made certain that news of his arrest does not leak out."

"Why has he got to go to the hospital?"

"My nephew hit him. Broke his jaw."

"Good heavens, what did he hit him with?"

"An upper cut. He used to box for his university."

Obruensi laughed. "Well, that's one way to get patients. Break 'em up then put 'em back together again, eh? Jolly good."

Quarshie's hand was in a plaster cast and Mrs. Quarshie was soaping him down under the shower in their home. Her activities soon led to developments in which they forgot Norenga and ended up blissfully asleep in each other's arms.

CHAPTER THIRTEEN

". . . le maître chanteur, *blackmailer*."

"I've got the superintendent behind bars. He is a very angry man. Had to arrest him at the point of a gun," Iyrini told Quarshie when the latter arrived, after an early start, back at the Norenga Police Station the following afternoon. He had dropped Mrs. Quarshie at the rest house on his way through town. "Want to go and talk with him? Though I don't suppose you'll get much out of him except snarls. He's like a tiger in there."

Another tiger in red weather? Quarshie wondered. He did not want to waste time looking at a caged tiger. He said so.

"Good. Well, for a start, a squad has been posted at the man Temple's hideaway. They will pick up anyone who strolls in there. There is no sign of the young chief. I know him personally, by the way. He is a tricky customer. As for the Frenchman, I set a guard around his house. I thought it would be better if you were there when I arrest him. His car is in the drive and he has not been seen in the compound all day. Shall we go and pick him up?"

The bungalow was a little way out of town. It had a high wall around it pierced by a single wrought-iron gate. The building was unfinished and obviously very recent. Because it was on the northern hillside above the valley it had a limited water supply which was fed from the river at the bottom of the hill by its own pump. With no water to waste, the compound was as dry and empty of vegetation as the neighbouring desert.

Iyrini spoke with the sergeant in charge of the guard in Hausa. "Have you had sight of the man since you last reported?" he asked.

"All I have seen, *dono,* that moved were some vultures. See, they are still there." He pointed up into the sky where in the evening light several of the great birds swung lazily like mobiles in a faint draught. "You said not to go inside, *dono,* or I would have investigated. Perhaps there is a dead dog in there, or some other offal. We looked over the wall but could not see anything."

Iyrini, who was lightly built, a wiry man with a very black skin and a most immaculate uniform, moved quickly to the gate. "I think we had better take a look, Doctor. Stay here, Sergeant, and make certain no one comes in," he told his subordinate. There was a sense of urgency in his words that proved to be justified when they walked through the house, which was open, to the rear verandah.

Quarshie knew at once what Martha's body must have looked like to the old hunter when he first found it.

René Dupré, or André Grevier, or whatever his true name might have been had suffered the same fate that she did. He appeared to have been stoned to death. The rocks with which his body had been pelted still lay around him on the floor of the verandah. More significantly there was a rifle, equipped with a telescopic sight, its butt soaked to the trigger guard in blood, lying beside him.

Slowly and emphatically Iyrini said, "We must be dealing with a manaic."

Quarshie did not speak for a long time. Then he said, "Or someone who wants to make us think we are. The man was killed, maybe with a blow from the butt of the rifle, then the body was stripped . . . see the shirt and pants are over there almost clean? Only after stripping did the killer go to work. Many murderers are mentally disturbed but few are as out of their minds as the mess here would suggest. And this man was behaving, at least in part, logically. Look, there is something else that bears that out. The killer was wearing shoes and stepped in the blood, noticed that he had left a print of the sole over there and took his shoes off . . . see? The next print in the dust is of a bare foot. That may or may not have been a very bright thing to do, but it does suggest that he was thinking coolly."

"Coolly enough to destroy the shoes afterwards?"

"Good question. My guess is that he was, or he hid them, or buried them."

"So we should not spend too much time looking for them?"

"Right."

"Then what can I do to help?"

For the moment, though he had heard the question, Quarshie ignored it. He said, "It was the roof of the verandah, the railings around it and your men outside the wall that discouraged the vultures. I imagine the birds instinctively want to have space around them for a clear takeoff when there are people nearby. If this man had been killed yesterday the vultures would have gotten to him because there were no guards to frighten them off. When did you put your men on duty up there?"

"We got to Norenga at nightfall yesterday. The men were here by eight this morning."

"Then he was killed last night or very early this morning. So, here is what you can do to help. He must have had a house boy. Find him. That's number one. Number two, beg, borrow or steal a large ground sheet and bring it in here. We'll cover this . . . this mess with it. Keep the guards outside. I don't want anyone to come in here at all. There is a good chance that only you, I and the murderer know that the man is dead. I want to keep it that way."

Iyrini saluted. "Yes, Doctor," he said and smiled, "you give orders like a military man, sir."

Quarshie shook his head. "You'll forgive me if I say that that is something I have never wanted to be. But I find it a pleasure to work with you, Captain. As Major Obruensi said, I believe we make a good team. While you go ahead with what I asked you to do, I will take a look around the house."

After Iyrini departed Quarshie stood for a while staring down at the Frenchman, wondering about the feelings of a man who could have so viciously destroyed another human being. As in Martha's murder the back of the skull had been smashed by a heavy blow and Quarshie's guess that it had been caused by the rifle was borne out when he examined the gun more closely. Besides blood there were particles of scalp and hair attached to it.

From the Frenchman's remains Quarshie turned his attention to the man's house. It was sparsely furnished and equipped in a way which suggested that the man who lived in it was nomadic. In fact, it appeared to be very little more than a campsite with the man's possessions piled on the floor as they might have been in a tent. The only item of furniture that had a look of permanency was the wide double bed. Seating was provided by sack-like canvas slings which were suspended from the roof beams.

Gingerly Quarshie lowered his bulk into one of them and found it both safe and comfortable. He doubted that an experienced criminal like René Dupré, alias André Grevier, alias . . . ? Quarshie decided to call him "Monsieur X." He doubted that Monsieur X would leave much in the way of casual evidence of any criminal activities around unless he were ridiculously overconfident. Though it was obvious that he could have been overconfident, because he had let a man holding a gun stand behind him and strike him down with it. Who? Foremost on the list of suspects must be his accomplices in the slaving business. Shirley, who had been in Port St. Mary at the time the murder had been committed, had to be ruled out.

Perhaps the superintendent, but he also had already been under arrest when Monsieur X had been poleaxed and battered.

Did the fact that the killing looked as if it had been the work of the same hand which had terminated Martha's life have any significance? Possibly, or, as he had already suggested to Iyrini, it could have been a deliberate subterfuge.

The gun? If it belonged to the murderer he would not have left it behind. So it had belonged to Monsieur X, if he was the French ambassador's man, who was so good with a *carabine*. It needed expertise to use a telescopic sight.

Whoever had tried to kill him, Quarshie, out in the desert when he had been looking for evidence had been an expert rifleman.

What had the old hunter said? The man he had seen had had

a very black face. "Your skin and mine, *dono,* even when we are not sweating, shines. The skin of that man did not shine. . . ." Because it had been dyed black? The old man had also said, "It seemed that the whites around his eyes were very large like those of a madman."

It was difficult, if not impossible, to dye the inside of one's eyelids and perhaps Monsieur X had left his eyelashes their natural blond colour. At a distance that would have given the impression of exceptionally wide whites of a man's eyes.

So? So Monsieur X could have been the gunman in the desert. Why was he seeking to kill Quarshie at that time? Was the fact that he had been sent up to Norenga to find Martha's murderer sufficient motive? That would have been a bit wholesale, no? But the trail he was following could have led to discoveries which would have pointed to the slave trading.

What had he found so far? (a) The gold in the hairbrush. (b) That he was following the same route which had led Martha, before him, to Shirley's hideaway.

Had Martha's visit to Shirley prompted Monsieur X to kill her? If that was the case why had he been murdered, himself, in the same manner that had been used to kill Martha? Monsieur X would have used his gun to execute Martha. He was used to killing. He would not have made a messy job of it by using a shovel, or some other blunt instrument. Unless . . . unless, he, too, was using his methods as a subterfuge.

Quarshie shrugged; perhaps he was constructing mysteries within mysteries.

But . . .

But he had only been looking at the fragments of evidence he had found, or thought he had found. Maybe something he had not found held the key—the papers, for instance, that had been missing from Martha's desk. If they were important enough to have been removed they must contain evidence that would be incriminating. He decided to look through the few boxes and other items which were stacked neatly around him on the floor.

Getting out of the hammock-like chair was not as easy as getting into it. He found he had to balance himself with his knees bent and his feet under him and push the canvas away behind him with his hands.

He searched for some twenty minutes before finding anything which interested him. He was a man on the move, or always prepared to move: he kept nothing he did not need. There were several books that were interleaved with currency notes in high denominations from a variety of countries. A simple hiding place for money in an almost illiterate neighbourhood. Clothes; he was obviously meticulous about his appearance and . . . the one item Quarshie found interesting. A magazine, published by a university press, on archaeology. In the table of contents listed on the cover there was an article written by Sir Percival Courtney-Beauchamp, K.C.M.G. It was entitled "New Insights into the Ancient Gold Trade in Mali." Quarshie thumbed through a few pages and found references to names like al Mus'udi, Ibn Hawga and Ibn Abi-Zar as well as many others. Then he was surprised to find loose photocopies of two handwritten letters. Both were addressed to "Dearest Antoine," and both carried dates which suggested that they had been written well over twenty years before Monsieur X's death. Antoine? Another René Dupré alias?

They were both highly emotional love letters, the second one starting, "I can't tell you how excited and happy I am to be able to tell you that I am going to have a baby, your baby." The letter was signed "Christine." Clipped to the bottom of the last one was an obituary notice which announced the "untimely death of Lady Christine Courtney-Beauchamp in childbirth."

As he considered these pieces of paper Quarshie, for the first time since he had started working on the case, felt really sick at heart. He thought that it was now possible to add to the other criminal qualifications which the French ambassador had listed against Monsieur X *le maître chanteur,* blackmailer. His victim, or perhaps only one of his victims, being the old chief commissioner, Percy. It also provided the old man with an inescapable motive for wanting Monsieur X dead, whether he killed him himself, or whether he hired a killer to take advantage of the fact and method of Martha's death.

As Quarshie leant slackly against a doorpost considering the implications of this discovery he was surprised to hear Mrs. Quarshie's voice calling for him urgently.

He walked through to the front of the house and saw her standing at the gate backed by the Afro-Americans, the Smiths.

When she saw him she called, "Quarshie, I have to talk to you, so do the Smiths. The captain told me you were here, but this man"—she indicated the sergeant—"won't let me in and I can't make him understand anything and he won't even try to understand, either." She was indignant.

Quarshie walked down to the gate and spoke through it, "What is so urgent?" he asked. He was still under the influence of the discovery which had put Percy firmly on the list of suspects and he could not, for the moment, think of anything else as more important.

"Only that they want to confront that man, that Frenchman who lives here, in front of you. He's a blackmailer. He has been trying to blackmail them. He has been selling them gold pieces, like the ones I found in Martha's hairbrush, and now he is threatening to expose them for buying gold. He says he is a representative of some international group set up to catch people who indulge in illicit traffic in gold."

Sharply, now, Quarshie asked, "When did he make those threats?"

"Yesterday," Trenton said. "He came and saw us yesterday. He said he was being recalled to Europe to report and that he would keep quiet about our dealings with him if I paid him, in American dollars, five hundred bucks."

Quarshie said, "You have come too late."

"What do you mean? He's gone?"

"How did you react when he asked you for the money?"

"I could have killed him."

"But you didn't."

"Of course not, man. What's the matter with you? I come to you with important information and you ask me dumb questions."

Quarshie said in Hausa, "All right, Sergeant. This lady is my wife. She was sent to see me with these two people by Captain Iyrini."

For a moment the man hesitated and Quarshie added, "He is a big man, your captain, but I am a bigger one. He takes orders from me. Ask him when he comes back."

"Yes, *dono*."

The man opened the gate.

As the small group trooped up to the house Quarshie said softly, "I am going to take you to see your man, René, the Frenchman. He's dead and what you will find is very, very ugly, maybe frightening. Of course, you don't have to come with me if you don't want to. You can just take my word for it, that he is dead, murdered."

Mrs. Quarshie suddenly lost her attitude of indignation and self-importance and stood motionless on the path.

The others stopped with her.

Trenton said, "I'm sorry, man. I guess I . . ." He ran out of words.

Terri asked, "Who killed him? Did you catch him?"

Quarshie shook his head. He said, "Prudence, you and Terri had better sit on the front verandah, here." To Trenton he said, "I think, unless you feel very strongly otherwise, that you should come with me."

Trenton said, "Yessir," and bowed his head.

A few moments later, as he stood looking down at the terrible sight on the edge of the back verandah he said, "Holy God."

CHAPTER FOURTEEN

"Can you prove to me that you did not kill him, or have him killed?"

Sir Percival Courtney-Beauchamp sat staring down at the cover of the archaeological magazine that Quarshie had just handed him.

The pressure lamps were hissing in the background but not loudly enough to interfere with the last movement of Mahler's *Das Lied von der Erde*. Perhaps Percy was thinking of Bruno Walter's statement about the work which was on the sleeve of the record. He had written that ". . . here, while the world sinks slowly away, the 'I' becomes the experience itself . . . a limitless range of feeling opens for him who soon will leave this earth."

As Percy thumbed through the pages of the magazine and came, as Quarshie had intended he should, accidentally on the photocopies of the letters, the past caught up with him and perhaps hurried him a few more steps towards his leave-taking from "this earth."

The old man's hands were quite steady but his face turned grey.

Quarshie waited for him to say something. It took a long time.

Finally, in a clear and level voice, Percy asked, "Where did you find these?"

"Amongst the effects of a Frenchman who called himself René. Perhaps you knew him as Antoine?"

"I did, a long time ago. Amongst his effects you say, then he has escaped, run away?"

"In a sense he has escaped if what was pursuing him was justice. He is dead. I found the magazine and the papers in his room."

"How did he die?" Percy's voice was suddenly much weaker.

Quarshie got up, poured a stiff whiskey and gave it to him. The old man sipped it slowly and Mrs. Quarshie restrained

an impulse to go and take his gnarled hand. She felt he needed
more help than whiskey could give him.

She said, "Whatever all this is about . . . I . . . I am on
your side."

Percy turned towards her with a slightly puzzled frown which
cleared when their eyes met and he said, "Those could be the
kindest words anyone has ever spoken to me, madam. Thank
you." To Quarshie he said, "You understand what this means?"

"The letters were being used to blackmail you?"

Percy took his time before he answered. "It's quite a long
story. But you did not reply when I asked you how he died?"

"He was murdered and it was made to look as if the same
man who killed Martha also killed Monsieur X."

"Monsieur X?"

"He had many aliases and had committed many crimes. The
French Deuxième Bureau wanted him."

"And how was his death made to look like Martha's murder?
Why don't you think it was done by the same man? Does your
statement mean that you know who committed the first
murder?"

"Do you mind, sir, if I ask the questions?"

"Of course, since you know, now, that I may have had a motive for killing Antoine, your Monsieur X, I must be treated as
a suspect."

Quarshie moved uncomfortably in his chair and Mrs.
Quarshie said, "My husband is a very honest and a very fair
man, sir."

"I know, madam. Forgive me. This has all been a very great
strain and I am . . . old."

Again Mrs. Quarshie felt the impulse to pat his hand and
make sympathetic noises but restrained it.

"Perhaps if you could tell me the story behind those documents it would help," Quarshie suggested.

Percy turned the magazine with his article in it in his hands
and glanced again at the letters.

"It may surprise you to learn," he said eventually, "that
Monsieur X had an evil hand in both the article and the letters.

Somehow he came by those same pieces of gold that you showed me on Christmas Day. So you must have been close on his tail, even then. Were you? Sorry. I forgot. I am on the witness stand." He took a sip of whiskey and continued. "He brought the gold pieces to me. And he told me a story about how he had found them. Then he took me to the place where he told me he had dug them up. He also showed me a few more artifacts which could have authenticated his dig. We experts are very gullible, you know. Did you ever read about Piltdown man? One of the cleverest hoaxes of all time and its perpetrator is still unknown. Or the work of that Dutchman, Van Meegeren? He fooled the best of the connoisseurs and specialists with a whole range of work in the style of a variety of great classical painters. Monsieur X fooled me. That gold you have is the real thing. Where he got it from I don't know. But it was not from what he showed me as his dig.

"You say the French police are after him for a host of crimes. This was his neatest and may well have been his most profitable. He made castings of the real gold medals in some kind of metal alloy of the right weight and then had them plated in gold. There are lots of craftsmen in Ghana and half a dozen other countries who could have done it for him. That was simple. But he had to overcome the suspicions of people who knew something about the business. I was the man who did that for him. He fooled me, with the evidence he showed me, into thinking that his stories of his find were genuine. Then, since he said no one would believe him if the find was his he persuaded me, for quite a handsome fee, that it was in my interest to claim to have been the finder. Who would question the story if I told it as my own? No one did. From an archaeological point of view it was not an earth-shaking one. But it served Monsieur X's purpose beautifully.

"Fool. I am speaking of myself." He had been speaking bitterly. Now his voice became harsh and vicious. "And cuckold. He seduced my wife. As the obituary says she died in childbirth. A daughter. His daughter. She survived her mother's death. My daughter, now. However, whatever else I have to say about Antoine, one has to admit that he was intelligent. So is my daughter. She has a good research grant in archaeology, a subject she took up because it was the one in which I could help her most. She is working, now, on a project in the Indus Valley." He sighed and concluded. "I think you can tell the rest of the story, Doctor."

"Some of it, sir. Monsieur X could have destroyed your reputation and your daughter's life. Did you destroy his life?"

"It would not have mattered if he had exposed me as a fraud, even if that could be proved only in the one instance. But my daughter. She is doing good work, I tell you. I am proud of what I have made of her and of what she has made of herself. For her sake I should have destroyed him, or had him destroyed years ago. I did not. And I have had no hand in what has happened to him now."

The record on the old man's incredible record player came to an end and he got up and turned it off.

When he sat down again he asked, "Assuming you catch the man who did the murder . . . your Monsieur X, how much of what I have told you will have to come out?"

"Can you prove to me that you did not kill him, or have him killed?"

"The answer to the first part of your question is that, if he was killed within the last two days, yes I can prove I am innocent because I have not moved from this house in that time and I have a half-dozen employees who could swear to that. Ask around without telling them why you are asking. You'll get honest answers. So far as the second part of the question, did I have him killed, I can swear to you I did not but you can prove that I didn't only by finding the man who did. May I say that, having seen you and this sweet and admirable lady here at work, I have every confidence that you will find him. So let me ask again. If you find that I am not connected with murder, as its instigator or as perpetrator, how much of what I have told you will need to come out?"

Quarshie thought for a moment and replied. "I think we understand each other, sir, and that you realise that circumstances are rather different here than what they might be in North America, or Europe. The newspapermen in this country are not as highly trained, or highly paid, to uncover information that makes headlines and destroys people who have done little or no harm to others. What you have told me and my wife will remain a confidence that will be disclosed only if it helps us to identify the murderer, or murderers. I can give you no guarantees beyond that."

"And I would not ask for them, Doctor. I am innocent of murder, or having instigated it. And, though some may believe that I am old and cynical, I have not lost my faith in the belief that, in a case like this, if a man is truly innocent his innocence will be proved."

CHAPTER FIFTEEN

"My mastah walk like some man he get no shadow, sah."

Mrs. Quarshie awoke with a sense of foreboding. She took a cold shower to flush it out of her mind but there was nothing that she could identify and verbalise so the anxiety would not leave her. She wanted to tell Quarshie about the way she felt, but didn't know what to say.

It was typical of their relationship that she did not have to say anything. He spoke her thought. "This is going to be a difficult day," he told her as they walked to the car. "When you think the end of an exercise like this is in sight you have to be particularly cautious."

Mrs. Quarshie relaxed. He, too, was aware of the threat and would be careful.

As they were driven past the mosque the muezzin was using a bullhorn, which made his voice sound tinny and artificial, to call the faithful to prayer. "Won't be long before they are using tape recorders for that job," grunted Quarshie.

"When machines can do everything men can do, sah, what men going to do then?" Sergeant Major Ikwasti Johnson wanted to know.

"There will be war between the men and the machines."

"And how soon dat war going to begin, sah?"

"That will depend on how long it takes men to realise that they are born short-sighted and need to look into the distance."

"If it come, it goin' to be a bad war, sah?"

Quarshie was not prepared to make the effort to carry the conversation any further. "Who knows?"

The talk of war reawoke the sense of foreboding in Mrs. Quarshie. She felt it was ominous. She said, "I prefer to be woken by cocks crowing rather than by muezzins."

"That is because you are not Muslim, moddah," the sergeant major told her over his shoulder.

It was only a short journey from the rest house to the hospital.

Dr. Levitsky came into the hospital grounds close behind them. He and Mrs. Quarshie were to make a round of bush clinics because his own midwife was still awaiting the birth of her child.

Levitsky behaved either as if he was in a hurry or as if he wanted to avoid any personal contact with Quarshie. He parked just in front of them, jumped out of his car, waved to the doctor and called to Mrs. Quarshie, "I'll be with you in a couple of moments. I have to pick up some reports from pathology. They came in last night from Port St. Mary."

Mrs. Quarshie got out of their car and told her husband, "Don't wait. But . . . but please take care. Look after him, Sergeant Major. He is a very important man."

"He safe wid me, moddah. He more than important, he is the mostest important of all."

Mrs. Quarshie made an effort and smiled.

Quarshie said, "Don't worry, Prudence. By tomorrow, or the next day, we shall be on our way home."

His words carried through the open window nearby to Levitsky as he searched through the papers on his desk. They caused him to pause for a moment. But he did not look up.

Iyrini was at his morning prayers on the verandah in front of his office at the police station when Quarshie arrived. The doctor walked past him without interrupting him and sat down to wait.

Iyrini completed his devotions, rolled up his prayer mat and came to the door.

Quarshie stood up, put his hands together in front of him and said, "*Salaam-u-alleikum.*" He was smiling.

Iyrini returned the smile and the salutation before he said, "I think I have some useful information for you, Doctor. I found the Frenchman's servant without much difficulty. He told me that yesterday his master gave him the afternoon off and that as he was walking away from the bungalow he saw the D.O. driving up towards it. I sent a man around to the back to ask the cook if the D.O. was home. He said he was but that he was ill and staying in bed."

"That's interesting. I will call and enquire after his health. What time was it when the servant saw him on his way to visit our man?"

"I did not ask."

"Never mind, it's not important. I hope you will do as well with the next job I have for you. You said you knew this young chief who was working with Temple?"

"Alhaji Baba Fagaci, yes."

"Do you think you could somehow get a message to him that Temple wants to see him? Make it sound conspiratorial. Someone in his family must know where he is. If we managed to keep the Englishman's removal to Port St. Mary as quiet as I think we have it should be possible to have Fagaci walk into the trap you will lay for him at the hideaway, right?"

"Yes, Doctor. I will do my best."

"Fine. Now, the sergeant major and I will pay a visit to the D.O."

Ephraim's face glistened with sweat.

Quarshie stood at the end of the bed looking down at him. He had asked the sick man for his symptoms.

"A terrible headache, buzzing in my ears"—he shrugged— "and you can see how I'm sweating."

"Did this start before or after you went to see René?"

"I haven't been to see him." The answer was returned very quickly and with emphasis. "Why do you say that?"

Quarshie stared expressionlessly down at the man but did not reply.

"Why do you think I've been to see René?"

Quarshie ignored that question, too. He asked, "Do you mind if I examine you? I mean, physically. If I can diagnose what's wrong I can probably prescribe something to help you get over it."

Ephraim said, "Of course. Go ahead . . . but why," he

persisted, "did you ask whether I got sick before I went to see René or after?"

Quarshie turned away. "Just a moment while I get my bag. And don't worry about my question because you have answered it."

Several minutes later he returned and the examination was thorough and included taking Ephraim's blood pressure.

When he finished he sat on the side of the bed looking wordlessly at his patient until Ephraim said, "Well?"

"Bit of tachycardia, blood pressure is up a bit, too. Any previous history of high blood pressure?"

"None that I know of."

"But you have been under a lot of stress, haven't you?"

"What do you mean?"

"Well you were telling us about the problems you have been having up here, remember? Being called a murderer because some of the old people died when they were moved away from the area where they are going to build the dam. And Percy's interference. And Martha. And your problems with the superintendent. Did he tell you, by the way, that René was blackmailing some of the people up here?"

"No." And as an afterthought, a bit hurriedly: "Who was he blackmailing?"

"Percy and the two Americans. I suspect that there were others."

"You say the superintendent told you that?"

"Yes."

"You know, if the man was blackmailing anyone I would have said it would have been the superintendent. They did not seem to be getting along together at all well recently."

Quarshie said, "I knew quite a bit about René's history before I came up here. He seems to have been a pretty nasty specimen."

"I did not like him much, but I knew nothing about him that would have suggested he was a blackmailer."

"So that wasn't the reason you went to see him yesterday afternoon?"

Ephraim screwed up his eyes and asked angrily, "What the hell is the matter with you? Being the big criminal investigator must be driving you out of your mind."

"Maybe it is. I had better be going. It is not good practice for a doctor to excite his patient, especially when he has high blood pressure. Look, I'm going to leave some tablets here. They'll relax you, help to bring down that blood pressure. They'll taste a bit sharp. Take a couple now and a couple in three hours' time." He put the bottle down beside the tablets. "Oh, and no alcohol, right? Not unless you want to put out the light for good. One has to be careful with hypnosedatives, you know, barbiturates and things like that. Don't take more than I have prescribed and no alcohol."

The sergeant major was waiting for Quarshie in the car.

"Drive round the corner out of sight," the doctor told him, "then tell me what you have found out."

A couple of minutes later:

"It was like what you said, sah. The cook he talk with the district officer, sah, before he go out. Dat time, the big man wearing his shoes. The cook he here when the D.O. come back. When he came from his car, sah, he never get shoes."

Quarshie received this information in silence. After he had sat with his eyes shut for quite a long time he sighed and said, "I want you to stay here, Sergeant Major, keep the house under observation. But first I want you to let the air out of the tyres on the front wheels of the D.O.'s car. You know how to do that?"

"Yes, sah."

"Good. Then, if the D.O. comes out, I don't think he will, but if he does, follow him. It does not matter if he sees you. If he goes to some house, or bungalow, stay and watch again. I will tell the captain to send another man to join you. You will use him for a messenger. Send him to the captain to tell him where you are. Understand?"

"Yes, sah. Where you goin', sah? Moddah say I mus' look after you."

"To Dr. Levitsky's house and I don't think that will be any more pleasant than my visit here."

The sergeant major said, "Yes, sah," as a matter of habit, not because he knew what Quarshie was talking about.

In front of Dr. Levitsky's house there was a small patch of coarse grass struggling against suffocation in the dusty soil. There was also a flower bed with a few scarlet cannas in it. In another bed half a dozen zinnias sat in the centre of an uncertain ring of stunted french marigolds. In all it was a sad little plot of land which spoke of failure, presenting itself as the evidence of Hanna Levitsky's childlike endeavour to fight a battle she could never win.

The bungalow, with its high semicircular verandah, stood above and behind the "garden," an ancient bastion that had been constructed in another age to combat the encroaching tide of sand flowing remorselessly south from the Sahara.

As Quarshie mounted the curving outside staircase Hanna came to meet him at the top step.

"But what a nice surprise, Doctor," she said. "I heard your car. Of course you would know, because my husband is out with your wife, that I would be alone. Poor Hanna is often alone. But not today, not now. Since you are come I am very happy."

The silent fire of the sun burned the back of Quarshie's neck. Standing in his shadow, Hanna Levitsky looked up at him, her blue eyes wide, her red hair still in a pony tail but, at her temples, plastered to her skin with sweat.

"Come inside." She held out a hand to lead him into the comparative darkness of the jalousie-windowed lounge.

It was here that the Christmas tree had stood. Now, without its candles and decorations, the circular space, sparsely filled with government-issue furniture, looked drearily commonplace.

Mrs. Levitsky said, "I hate this room. I have my own. Hanna's room. Usually I don't take people there but it's where I entertained Martha when she came to see me and since you have come to talk about Martha surely that is where we should go."

Quarshie restrained an impulse to ask her how she could be so positive about the reason for his visit. However, he welcomed the opportunity to talk with her in surroundings in which she might feel comfortable. He was afraid the sterility of the big room would inhibit her.

From the world of defeated horticulture and heartless, stock-pattern lounge chairs and settees the setting into which Mrs. Levitsky led him spoke of her as unguardedly as she spoke of herself.

The main features which proclaimed her troubled nature were the paintings covering the walls and the clashing colours that were on display in the rest of the furniture. They made an indiscriminate mosaic in which most of its meaning was in its meaninglessness.

This was not true, however, of the individual paintings themselves. The hand which had created them had no more than childish skills but the mind which had conceived them revealed its torment. They were full of dimly perceived and half-realised nightmares built more of shadows than of substance in which pale, feminine images were threatened by others which were voraciously masculine. What, more clearly seen, might have been a field of flax in bloom was menaced by a dark shape which might have been a bulldozer. Something like a small bird cowered in the shadow of a much bigger bird that might have been an eagle. Diaphanous shadowy material was threatened by pinking scissors with enormously exaggerated teeth. In the simplest piece of symbolism, and the most clearly seen, a pattern of more or less concentric ovals was menaced by a piston, the latter having been cut out of another picture and pasted into the composition.

"Sol encourages me to make my pictures and Martha always said that she found them most interesting. She was a wonderful woman"—three "W's" in a row pronounced as three "V's"—"so strong."

"Your husband is a very good doctor, a very good doctor indeed." Quarshie felt the need to combat the image of Martha as "wonderful" and "strong." He had learned too much about the American woman to let Mrs. Levitsky's statement go uncontradicted.

For a while neither of them spoke, then Mrs. Levitsky said, "He is a man." It was stated as her reason for being critical of him.

"You mean like other men?"

"Yes, like other men."

"If that is what you think you are deceiving yourself. He is much better than most and you know it."

"Yes. I know it. But that does not change him from being a man, does it?"

In an effort to hide his irritation Quarshie decided to look at some of her paintings more closely.

"How much do you know about me?" Mrs. Levitsky spoke to Quarshie's back and her question was put as innocently as a child might have put it.

"One can never know very much about anyone. I know some things about you, the sort of things people call facts. But they are like the objects one might expect to see floating on the surface of a pond. What is underneath them is something you have to guess about."

"What are your guesses about me?"

"That your husband loves you . . . and that you don't love him."

"He is a man." She repeated the words patiently as if she was explaining something to someone who could not understand what the words meant. "To poor Hanna he is a man."

"And Martha?"

"She was strong. I loved her."

Quarshie felt an urge to curse the dead woman. He controlled the impulse and asked quietly, "What would have happened to you if your husband had not come along when he did and you had been left with the other survivors from the concentration camp?"

"He is a man, a good man. You said so." She felt enough shame to protest a little.

"But you loved Martha?"

"Yes. I was right to love her. She said I was."

"You told her everything about yourself?"

"Everything. She was always asking me questions."

"When she came here the last time did she give you anything?"

"Yes, papers. She said she knew they would be safe with poor Hanna."

"What was on the papers?"

"Lots of numbers. Why would she want to keep lots of numbers?"

"And where are the papers now?"

"In Sol's safe at the hospital. Martha said they were important. I asked Sol what I should do with them to be sure they did not get lost."

"Did your husband know that you loved Martha?"

"We never talked about it."

"Did Martha love you?"

"Yes. She said she did, often."

"And Marja and Mishka?" Quarshie was being deliberately cruel.

Hanna stiffened and closed her eyes.

"She . . . she said she loved them, too."

"Did she ask questions about other things? I mean other than questions about you. Did she ask about gold, for instance?"

Hanna shook her head.

"She asked a lot of questions about Dachau. She kept on asking them. She often repeated the same questions. She would look at my paintings, too, and ask me to explain them over and over again."

"She deserved to die."

"No, no. You must not say that. You don't know anything about her."

"You do?"

"We loved each other, that I know. And I know that when she held me I felt that no one could hurt poor Hanna anymore."

She was two people, Quarshie thought. "Poor Hanna," the mother of Marja and Mishka and a woman who needed a garden and other conventional adjuncts to her life.

"Did your husband ever hurt you?"

"He is a man."

"But did he ever hurt you?"

"No."

"Didn't you realise that what that woman was doing was going to destroy you and destroy everything your husband had tried to do for you?"

"She is dead and I don't want to talk about her anymore."

"And who killed her?"

"Sol."

"No. You did." Quarshie's anger left him. "I'm sorry. I am unkind. Poor Hanna."

"Yes, poor Hanna. After you go I shall cry for poor Hanna. And you must go soon because now you know everything about me and about Sol that you want to know. Yes?" She spoke brightly with her head on one side.

Quarshie nodded, thinking, in fact, that he knew far too much about everybody in Norenga. The condition he had found there had been cancerous and growing all the time.

He said very softly, "How brutal the world can be to people who have never hurt anyone else." He was thinking that when Sol had rescued Hanna the pathology of her condition would already have suggested that it might be terminal. She had been too brutally injured ever to recover and his anger was diverted towards the guards in the concentration camp and the people responsible for the camp's instigation. They represented the worst of the destructive forces in men, a plague for which there are still no adequate antibodies.

"Perhaps we cannot prevent this world from being one in which children are tortured. But we can reduce the number of tortured children." Only if we get there in time, Quarshie

thought, and can protect them from others, like Martha, who
. . . in whatever cause . . . are prepared to commit the same
atrocities.

He stood up.

Hanna sat still, her eyes wide again, staring at him intensely.
Presently she, too, stood up and held out her hand to him, as
she had when he arrived, but now the gesture was more tenta-
tive, as if she was afraid he might rebuff her.

When he took her hand she said, "You are a good man, like
Sol. But is it enough to be so good when many others are so
bad? I wonder. Come . . . how is it they say it? I will see you
off the premises."

Ephraim lay sprawled on his face across his bed.

The sergeant major said, "Is he dead, sah? I never hear
nothing from the house. I watch and watch. Nobody come,
nobody go. At all."

Quarshie turned the D.O. on his back and the fumes of alcohol on his breath enveloped the doctor and made him turn his
head to one side. When he raised the patient's eyelids he found
the man's pupils dilated. Ephraim was muscular but when
Quarshie moved his limbs they were as limp and flaccid as if
the stuffing had gone out of them.

Quarshie said, "Drunk. There must be an empty bottle
around somewhere."

"Dis medicine bottle, heah, dey be empty, sah."

"Yes, I noticed that."

"And dis bottle"—the sergeant major picked it up—"whiskey
bottle, for underside the bed, sah"—he held it upside down—
"catch nothing for inside."

"Fine. Now the next thing is to find the car keys."

"Dey here, sah, for dis table."

"Good. Now, if you had a car and a pair of shoes that you
did not want anyone to find, but you were in a hurry, where
would you put them?"

"I tink so, sah, maybe I go put 'em for back side de car."

"Take the keys, then, and go and look."

When the sergeant major had gone Quarshie sat down on the bed beside the inert Ephraim.

For quite a while he stared at his unconscious, one-time teammate before he spoke to him. Then he said, "Well, my friend, this could be the end of the line. You killed René, didn't you?

"Why?

"Jealousy?

"I don't think so. You got worked up over something else or he had some information he was using to blackmail you. The man's racism, perhaps, might have upset you, too. The way he looked at your black skin and the way he treated you and spoke to you. We will talk about all that tomorrow. Meantime you got taken in by what we both used to call a sucker punch. You let yourself be drawn right onto it." He picked up the empty medicine bottle. "Vitamin C in a barbiturate's bottle. You thought I had offered you a way out. Too bad I could not do just that. But my job is difficult enough without having to play the role of judge, jury and executioner as well." He paused. "And what about Martha? You did not kill her, did you? So who did? Intuition has been telling me the answer to that question for a long time. Soon, I am afraid—and I really mean I am afraid—I am going to find out whether my instinct was correct." He examined the cast on his right hand. "I should have known better than to go for a knockout with a naked fist. You could have told me that, I know. But that event was like everything which has happened on this case. Every surprise I get is an ugly one."

He stood up and walked to the window.

Outside, in the blazing afternoon sunlight, there was a total stillness. Somewhere out there in the terrible heat, he thought, Mrs. Quarshie was doing her round of clinics with Dr. Levitsky. Very few other people anywhere in the neighbourhood would be working. Certainly no Europeans except the dedicated Sol. A great man who had run away, taking his skills, his dedication and his anguish, too, to what for him must have been the rim of the world. "There are so many people who have suffered as that man has," Quarshie mused. "And there are so many ways to try to escape that suffering. But you can still get cornered. Horror is like a steel bear trap, cruel and inescapable."

The sergeant major came in and Quarshie turned to face him.

"Catchum, sah." He held out the shoes. "Like we say, he dey for back side de car."

Quarshie took the shoes and turned them over so that he could examine the soles. Softly he said to Ephraim, "So the sucker punch set you up for a knockout."

"What's dat, sah?"

"An observation, my friend, that only the D.O. would understand." He looked at the bloodstains on the sole of one of the shoes again, then he put them both down. "Now here is what I want you to do, Sergeant Major. I want you to go back to the police station and tell Captain Iyrini that I have another man I want him to arrest. Say that he is a stretcher case. While you do that I will stay here with the . . . the suspect."

After the sergeant major had saluted and departed Quarshie turned to Ephraim again and said, "Sorry I have to do this, friend, but I have no choice."

A couple of hours later, after having seen a steel door locked on the still insensible D.O., Quarshie returned to the rest house to find that Mrs. Quarshie had gotten there ahead of him.

She was taking another cold shower. It was a procedure which Quarshie usually enjoyed watching. It evoked feelings which were sensuous and turned easily to sensual but he knew that they were not for today.

He could tell at a glance that Mrs. Quarshie was even more upset than he was by his trip to the jail with Ephraim, an action he had seen as being kindred to betrayal.

Mrs. Quarshie's unhappiness began to overflow the moment she came out of the shower and started to dry herself. Since her anxiety was greater than her sense of modesty, Quarshie had difficulty in keeping his mind on what she was saying.

"I would not have believed it if I had not seen it." There was a note of real incredulity in her voice. "He went raving mad. I thought he was going to kill the man."

"Who was going to kill what man?"

"Levitsky. He wanted to attack the father of a girl who was brought to the clinic suffering from severe haemorrhaging. She was seven or eight years old and following that disgusting old custom . . . men"—she interrupted herself to expostulate—"for centuries they have been monsters and in a large part of the world they still are . . . following tribal custom someone had attempted a clitoridectomy on the child and they must have been using a blunt knife or a piece of glass. I have seen some bad cases but this must have been as bad as the worst. Anyway, Levitsky went out of his mind and wanted to attack the man with a scalpel . . . to operate on him, he said, the same way he had tried to operate on the girl. The driver and I had to hold him back. And, Quarshie, he's strong. He was like a dog with rabies. I could not recognise him. The way that child had been mutilated seemed to fill him with unbearable pain. Really, it broke over him like a wild thunderstorm, black and terrible." Mrs. Quarshie was sitting on the bed beside her husband, now, with her knees up, drying between her toes. "He was in a funny sort of mood from the beginning of the day. I had a bit of the same feeling, as if there was a curse on it, bad *juju*. Has it affected you the same way?"

Quarshie told her about Hanna Levitsky and Ephraim.

"Oh no," she said when he had finished, "but why?" She was referring to the D.O.

"I don't know. Perhaps, when he sobers up, tomorrow, he will tell me."

Mrs. Quarshie got off the bed and tied a cloth around her. It had an intricate pattern of African masks on it in black on a very dark-red background. She crossed the top ends of the cloth over her breasts and tied them, with long ends which stood up, behind her neck. It was the traditional night attire of most African women.

"What else can happen today, Quarshie? If someone has put a curse on it there are still quite a few hours to go."

Quarshie did not answer her but if he had he would have expressed his feeling accurately by saying, "I don't know. Perhaps the worst is yet to come."

His apprehension was justified a little after midnight when they were both wakened by someone hammering on the jalousie shutters of their bedroom crying, "Mastah, mastah."

Quarshie had not been sleeping very deeply, perhaps because he was anticipating some sort of intrusion into his already restless night.

He opened the jalousie to find Levitsky's steward outside.

"Sah, sah," the man said frantically, "my mastah tell me ax you go come he house one time. Catch bad palaver, sah, bad palaver too much."

"What has happened?"

"I no sabbee, sah. My mastah walk like some man he get no shadow, sah." To say that a person casts no shadow is an African way of suggesting that he has become a ghost.

Quarshie said, "I come." And to his wife: "I don't know exactly what to expect, but whatever it is, it will be bad. Do you want to go with me?"

"Of course."

The note, which was lying on Levitsky's chest in an envelope addressed to Quarshie, read, "Sorry to get you out on a night call like this, Doctor, especially when, in the direct sense, there is nothing you can do. Indirectly, however, there is an immediate need. Someone is going to have to look after my patients in the hospital from this moment on. I know I can rely on you to take over.

"The keys with this note are for the poison cupboard, my surgery and the safe in my surgery.

"For the rest there is little to say. My outburst this afternoon and your conversation with my wife will have confirmed the suspicions you have had for a long time. You believed, from early on in our association, that I was both capable and guilty of Martha's death, but I knew that you could not prove it and that without proof you would not act. Rather you would go on waiting for the proof to come along. I could not go on waiting, knowing that you were getting closer all the time. You are a patient man; I am not. The main part of the proof you need, motive, is in the safe in my surgery. In a court of law what you find there might persuade a judge and jury to take a clement attitude. That would not be enough. The mere fact of my arrest and trial would destroy, or perhaps I should say, complete the destruction of Hanna. She could not live without me. I will not live without her.

"So, adieu, Quarshies both. If I had been looking for evidence that humanity is worth saving I would say that you two provide it and I am glad to have had you by me at the end as confidantes and, I hope, friends.

"Cause of death, Doctor? To save you the trouble of a P.M., air embolism, clean, fast and virtually painless."

Quarshie read the note aloud to his wife. When he looked up at her she was crying. Slowly he looked away from her towards Levitsky and his wife. They lay, side by side, on the bed, apparently asleep. It was a condition from which they would never wake again. An empty hypodermic syringe, the instrument which had caused their death, lay on the floor beside the bed.

CHAPTER SIXTEEN

"The dead are not dead."

It seemed to Mrs. Quarshie as if the whole population of Norenga had turned out for the Levitskys' funeral. It was behaviour that was customary when an important member of the community died. Powerful men were not buried without appropriate ceremony because if those left behind did not show their respect in a suitable manner the dead might come back and haunt them or allow themselves to be used by sorcerers for wicked purposes.

Levitsky, owing to the seeming miracle cures he had effected and his reputation for being a wise man, had been regarded as one of the most powerful men in the region. As for Hanna there were suspicions that, because of her red hair, she might have been a witch. So the propitiatory element in the respect the townspeople were showing was most sincere.

The funeral was being held on the barren hillside overlooking the river where Percy had told them earlier that his grave "had already been dug." He had offered the location to Quarshie, who had been asked to organise the last rites, as a burial site, saying, "There is plenty of room for the three of us and it will give me some companionship to look forward to. It could be lonely here as the one alien amongst all the other native spirits." The old man had not, however, offered to accommodate René Dupré in his plot. Monsieur X's remains had been interred, without any mourners, in a corner of his own barren compound. A large rock had been rolled on top of his grave to ensure that he stayed in it.

Quarshie and Percy now stood at the head of the hole in the ground which had been dug to take the two rather small coffins. They were the chief attendants at the funeral and while the drummers drummed and professional mourners wailed in subtle harmonies, the rest of those who had come to the funeral followed centuries of local tradition and filed past the doctor and the retired commissioner and offered their respect for the dead and small sums of money to help pay for the funeral expenses and the feasting and drinking which would follow as a regular part of the last rites.

Many of those who expressed their condolences did so by wishing Levitsky and his wife safe arrival in a "haven of fresh breezes," that being the most perfect destiny conceivable to people who lived on the harsh threshold of the biggest desert in the world. If they ever condemned anyone to hell they would have described it as a nether world of "broken pots," a place where there are no utensils in which to preserve the most precious substance in their world, water.

Another piece of ritual which Mrs. Quarshie, Trenton and Terri Smith had watched, from a slight rocky eminence some distance from and above the grave, had been the turning of the coffins, several times, in circles, so as to confuse the spirits of the dead and thus make it more difficult for them to return and haunt the region.

In tune with Mrs. Quarshie's thoughts Trenton Smith softly intoned a stanza of Birago Diop's famous poem:

> Those who are dead are never gone:
> they are in the thickening shadow.
> The dead are not under the earth:
> they are in the tree that rustles,
> they are in the wood that groans,
> they are in the water that runs,
> they are in the water that sleeps,
> they are in the hut,
> they are in the crowd:
> the dead are not dead.

And using the words the crowd kept chanting, he added, "He was a good man," and "She was a good woman," even though people's doubts about Hanna's true nature made the way the crowd paid their tribute to her memory a little less emphatic. Noticing the difference, Mrs. Quarshie thought, No one, except perhaps Levitsky, and certainly not the people of Norenga, could guess the kind of hell Hanna had been through.

The experiences Quarshie had undergone during the past few days, Mrs. Quarshie thought, had been comparable to a nightmare. Nor had it been an easy time for her. Now, with the scorching wind burning her lips and the fierce pressure of the sun on the back of her head and neck, they had come to the last act.

Turning back through her memories, she thought of Trenton's and Terri's admission that they had been planning to smuggle gold out of Akhana and that the lonely trips they had taken into the barren rock and scrub country outside the town had usually been for assignations with those who were prepared to trade with them for gold. It was in this way that they had gotten into René's hands and he had sold them three forged and valueless medallions like the genuine ones Mrs. Quarshie had found in Martha's hairbrush. From that sale René had started trying to blackmail them. After they made their confession to Quarshie he had thanked them and had told them that so far, in buying gold, they had committed no crime and that if they wanted to run risks smuggling it out at a later date that was none of his business but he advised against it. He also told them that he was going to turn the three genuine medallions that Mrs. Quarshie had found in Martha's hairbrush over to the state museum.

Watching some vultures circling high in the painfully brilliant, blue cupola of the sky, Mrs. Quarshie next thought of Iyrini's triumphant return from Shirley's hideaway with the young chief Alhaji Baba Fagaci, as he had put it, "in the bag," captured while in the process of bringing in more young women to be sold to Arab slavers.

Despite the heat, she felt a little shiver go up her spine when she remembered René Dupré trying to gun down Quarshie and crippling Yosofo, perhaps for life. The old hunter who had saved Quarshie from the assassin's bullet was prominent down in the crowd of mourners, using the occasion to show off the new gun Quarshie had bought for him. In explaining Monsieur

X's attack on him Quarshie had told her the Frenchman knew that, along the trail he was following to Martha's murderer, he would be bound to uncover either evidence of the man's black slaving or his activities as a *maître chanteur,* a blackmailer. Perhaps he would find evidence of both and therefore the Frenchman had tried to get rid of him.

Then, out of the jumble of Mrs. Quarshie's memories, came her impression of the local people's reaction to Sol Levitsky's suicide. To them there was nothing reprehensible about a man taking his own life. Traditionally it was seen as an act of protest, behaviour like that of the Buddhist priests Mrs. Quarshie had read about who had burned themselves alive as a protest against the continuing slaughter during the Vietnam war. Sol's protest, and it was one which he had made a part of the pattern of his life, was against "man's inhumanity to man," particularly when that inhumanity was directed against the young and the blameless. His death, therefore, for those who knew him, was the natural outcome of this concern. He had killed Martha to stop her doing further harm to Hanna and he had committed the murder when he had been under the control of a terrible all-consuming rage similar to the one which had taken hold of him the day Mrs. Quarshie had been touring his clinics. Curiously the incident which had sparked his fury then was one which had, on occasion, fired Martha as well.

Putting aside further thought of Martha for a moment, but intending to return to it, Mrs. Quarshie considered Ephraim's unhappy history. Quarshie had said that he had been suffering from having an overload of misfortune heaped upon him, one which, in addition to the initial misfortune of having an impulsive nature, had become too much for him to bear. He had impetuously fallen for Martha's blatant invitation to become her lover with, as an added attraction, the rewards she had offered him for his services. All this he had admitted to Quarshie in his confession. Thus, he said, he had played into Réné's hand and had given him one more victim to blackmail because Martha had, of course, talked of her liaison with Ephraim to the Frenchman, whom she had been using for her own purposes and from whom she must either have bought, borrowed or stolen the golden medallions.

In his profound contempt for all black people René had, however, become careless of their reactions to his attitude towards them. He had sneered at Ephraim and had taunted him about his relationship with Martha, telling him that she had joked about his sexual capabilities, calling him a "small boy" and saying that in bed "he was like an immature but sex-starved monkey." That was when René had turned his back on the object of his ridicule and Ephraim had picked up the rifle and had smashed the man's skull with its butt. It was a reaction, Quarshie had explained, which was due to the fact that he was on the point of a nervous breakdown from overwork and from the strain of his relationship with Martha. In addition, the D.O. had been given evidence that the superintendent was working hand-in-glove with Shirley, though without the policeman being aware that the Englishman was involved in a much bigger operation masterminded by René. Wheels within wheels, Mrs. Quarshie thought, and Ephraim had been afraid to expose the superintendent and Shirley for fear of what René might tell the government about his relationship and the money he was receiving from Martha to satisfy her lascivious appetite and to provide her with contacts with various people she wanted to talk with like Ladidi, the *magajiya*. There had followed Martha's murder and the Quarshies' arrival to investigate the affair.

So . . . Ephraim had done a pathetically efficient job of digging his own grave.

The drumming and the heat made the air quiver and Mrs. Quarshie wondered how her husband and the old white man, wearing an ancient khaki sun helmet, were able to breathe in the dust and the supercharged temperature amongst the closely packed bodies that surrounded them. The professional keeners, who were all women and had come in groups walking slowly in single file wailing and crying, broke their performance every now and then to say something in a normal voice to a neighbour before resuming their doleful cries. Most of the men,

dressed in the mourning colour of white, were silent and almost
motionless telling their prayer beads.

Mrs. Quarshie's ruminations came to an end with Martha.
The American woman's arrival on the scene had initiated the
process that had led, directly, to her own death and, indirectly,
to the Levitskys' suicide, to René's death and to the latter's at-
tempt on Quarshie's life.

Quarshie had spent almost every minute since he had been
called to the doctor's bungalow—and when he was not on duty
at the hospital—with the papers he had found in the safe at the
hospital. As he had expected, all the important notes had been
kept in code but he had been enormously helped by the fact
that Levitsky had broken it for him.

The code was typical, in its cleverness, of its inventor.
Martha had simply taken the typist's old standby of "the quick
brown fox jumps over the lazy dog" and given numbers to each
letter of the alphabet in the sentence in accordance with a completely random choice. What spark of insight, or genius, had
led Levitsky to his discovery was impossible to say, but whatever it was it deserted him when he had started to decode the
notes. Happenstance had decreed that the first entries he deciphered had related to Hanna. And he did not go any further.
The threat to his wife's tenuous hold on sanity posed by Martha's ruthless meddling was writ large in those first notes and
they engendered the fury which led to his tricking her with
some false gold into accompanying him out into the rocky waste
where he killed her. That was the conclusion which Quarshie
came to after he received an analysis from Port St. Mary of the
fingerprints on the shovel which had been used as the murder
weapon. Whether Levitsky had preplanted the false gold in the
crack of the rock, or had thrown it there and had invited
Martha to scrabble for it, was unimportant. The fact that she
had knelt down and offered him the back of her head was evi-
dent. At that moment he must have aimed a vicious downward
blow at his target with the side of the shovel. That the blade
had cut into her skull was indicated by the fact that traces of
brain tissue were found on it.

Quarshie's answer to Mrs. Quarshie's question about why Martha had been buried there amongst the rocks was that Levitsky had made an effort to hide his victim's body because, though it would have been more convenient to leave her remains to the vultures, their circling above the body and fighting amongst each other over it might have been visible from the road a couple of miles away and could, thus, have drawn attention to his "kill."

With that question answered all that remained to be revealed to Mrs. Quarshie was the contents of the section of the notes which Levitsky had not troubled to decode. It was unfortunate both for Martha and the Levitskys that the doctor had not taken his work of deciphering the documents Martha had left with his wife to their conclusion, for what he would have learned might conceivably have changed his attitude towards her.

Had he carried on he would have found, of course, material which would have underwritten his suspicions about what Martha had intended to do with the information she had collected about Hanna's history and the problems she and Levitsky had faced. It was going into a book. Nor would Levitsky have approved the ruthless way in which Martha used everyone, not only Hanna, to get material. She was a woman who quite clearly believed that it was permissible to use any kind of means to justify her ends. But the doctor would most probably have approved one of the ends she was working towards because it was in line with his most cherished ideal of reducing the number of tortured children in the world; though Martha's concern had not been for male children but only for the tortured females.

From Martha's notes, Quarshie had told his wife, it was clear to him that the American had attended, as an observer, a World Health Organisation conference held in Khartoum.

As an ardent feminist, albeit a rather unscrupulous one, she was planning a book which was going to bring before the world, as forcefully as possible, the report of that WHO Khar-

toum conference and set beside it her own findings in Norenga
and other parts of the Arab countries and Black Africa which
she had visited. The findings were that there are over thirty mil-
lion women in that part of the world, many of them young girls,
whose genitalia have been partly removed, sewn up, or infibu-
lated mainly at the behest of the male tribal elders and the old
women.

Mrs. Quarshie knew of the practice. What African woman
did not? Sexual mutilation of women was widespread in most
countries in Africa, with the possible exception of Algeria and
Libya. It was worst in Ethiopia, parts of the Sudan and Egypt.

Martha had dug out all the details. She had all the statistics
and the medical findings and thanks to her travels she could il-
lustrate them with precise case histories from her own research.

Why had she planned to include Hanna in such a book? To
show that women in Europe could be as bestially treated as
their sisters in Africa. It was a crusade which she had under-
taken and tragically it had come to an end on a rocky landscape on the southern fringes of the Sahara, at the hands of a
man who believed in some of the things she did but not in her
methods because he was personally involved and because neither gold nor financial profit motivated anything he did.

At the end, and it had been late on the evening of the day
which preceded the funeral before Quarshie had deciphered the
last word of the text, he had told Mrs. Quarshie, "Who can be
sure whether Levitsky's loving way of treating those who suffer
was better than Martha's, which was charged with hate but
might have had much greater impact than what he was doing?
We can only say which approach we, ourselves, prefer. The
choice? Patience, or impatience? To turn the other cheek or to
smite the enemy hip and thigh. The white man's Book offers us
both. What answer would you choose, Prudence?"

Her reply had been, "The same one you would choose,
Sam."

There had been no need for either of them to say anything
else.

At that moment in her ruminations Quarshie, from his position beside the grave, looked up towards her and, though she was a long way away, Mrs. Quarshie could see the sweat pouring down his face and soaking his white shirt.

It was an image which made her realise, as she did from time to time, that her love for him was great and that also, at that moment, she knew and shared his huge sense of pity for the man and woman in the wooden boxes which lay at his feet.